CAPTAIN GRINGO—ON TOP OF THE SITUATION

Captain Gringo slowly got out of the tub, careful not to splash or slosh. Whoever was ransacking his room might not know he'd been inside bathing. He slid his .38 from the shoulder holster he'd hung near the tub. Then, naked and still wet, he popped out of the john armed and dangerous.

The good-looking female burglar with the little nickel-plated pistol in her right hand was too slow. He dove at her in a flying tackle and disarmed her with his free hand as they fell together across the bed.

He had her pinned with his dripping upper torso crushed against her well-filled pongee bodice. His naked flesh could feel, through her now damp pongee, that whoever she was, she didn't wear anything under her tropic dress.

"Don't hurt me! I'll do anything you say!" she pleaded.

He grinned down at her and said, "You're so right."

Novels by
Ramsay Thorne

Renegade #1
Renegade #2: Blood Runner
Renegade #3: Fear Merchant
Renegade #4: The Death Hunter
Renegade #5: Macumba Killer
Renegade #6: Panama Gunner
Renegade #7: Death in High Places
Renegade #8: Over the Andes to Hell
Renegade #9: Hell Raider
Renegade #10: The Great Game
Renegade #11: Citadel of Death
Renegade #12: The Badlands Brigade
Renegade #13: The Mahogany Pirates
Renegade #14: Harvest of Death
Renegade #15: Terror Trail
Renegade #16: Mexican Marauder
Renegade #17: Slaughter in Sinaloa
Renegade #18: Cavern of Doom
Renegade #19: Hellfire in Honduras
Renegade #20: Shots at Sunrise
Renegade #21: River of Revenge
Renegade #22: Payoff In Panama

Published by
WARNER BOOKS

Renegade #22

PAYOFF IN PANAMA

Ramsay Thorne

A Warner Communications Company

WARNER BOOKS EDITION

Warner Books, Inc.,
666 Fifth Avenue,
New York, N.Y. 10103

A Warner Communications Company

Printed in the United States of America

First Warner Books Printing: January, 1984

10 9 8 7 6 5 4 3 2 1

Renegade #22

PAYOFF IN PANAMA

The boxom brunette on the bottom protested, "Oh, no! I couldn't! My dear departed husband explained on our wedding night how only the women of the lower classes make love completely naked!"

Captain Gringo didn't want to talk about her dear departed husband. He wanted her completely naked. He'd admired her black lace underwear, a lot, before she'd coyly trimmed her bedroom lamp and giggled into bed with him. But by now the stiff Spanish lace was becoming a pain in the ass, or, rather, an irritation to his own naked belly as she ground it against him. His bare ass was doing fine as they tortured the bedsprings together. For old Estralita, if that was her name, moved her ample hips with considerable skill and enthusiasm for a lady who seemed so worried about class distinctions.

Her bedroom shutters were open to catch the cooling trade

winds, of course, but it didn't help much. It was a sultry night for the Costa Rican high country, and the tall Yank's passion-flushed flesh was taking a beating from what now felt like sandpaper covering her otherwise voluptuous torso. It got worse when she started to bump and grind even harder, moaning, "Oh, querido! I am almost there again! Do it faster, por favor!"

He didn't. He stopped teasingly, still deep inside her, to insist, "This barbed-wire fence between us has to go, querida. Come on, I'll help you slip it off over your pretty little head like so and . . ."

"I do not wish for to be seen naked!" she protested, thrusting wildly with her hips as she weakly resisted his efforts to shuck her prickly rind. As he got the lace at least up around her shoulders and settled back against her now smooth, sensuous naked breasts, she gasped, moaned with pleasure, and gave in, saying, "Oh, it does feel nicer that way, no?"

Captain Gringo started moving in her again as he replied. "It feels better this way, yes indeed!" Then he tossed the damned fool lace aside, kissed her, and went crazy with her for a while.

When they came up for air at last, Estralita demanded her chemise back, saying, "The full moon is shining in on us from outside and, oh, Madre de Dios, we are both naked and ashamed! At least, I am ashamed. I know you men feel no shame about being naked but . . ."

He kissed her some more to shut her up as he ran his hands over her. When he cupped her privates in a friendly palm he assured her it was at least as good as a fig leaf. Estralita giggled and replied, "I do not think a fig leaf would feel as comfortable down there. But can you see my nipples in the moonlight? I can see even the hair on your chest, and, oh, what must you think of my character now?"

He held her closer, kissed her again, and assured her gallantly that his regard for her character hadn't changed. This was true enough. He still didn't know a hell of a lot about her.

He'd picked her up a little over an hour earlier at the San José paseo. The easy way. He'd been seated under the awning of a sidewalk cantina, nursing a tall gin and tonic as he waited to meet his sidekick, Gaston, when this boxom brunette had plopped down beside him and proceeded to tell him how much she missed her dear departed husband.

Since she'd been wearing a red satin flamenco outfit rather than the usual widow's weeds, Captain Gringo had assumed her husband had been dearly departed for some time and, from the way she'd batted her lashes at him, left her hurting for someone to fill the void.

He'd barely had time to leave a message at the cantina for Gaston before she'd almost dragged him by the hair up here to her apartamento. Now that they'd gotten the first shyness and that damned black lace out of the way, it was shaping up to be a lovely evening with a shapely lady indeed. Estralita was a little plump, but she had a pretty enough face and a really great way of moving those big hips. So, whatever Gaston had wanted to see him about could wait.

It was probably a job offer from someone who liked noise. Captain Gringo and his fellow soldier of fortune had been resting up between jobs in Costa Rica for some time now, and while the younger, American member of the team was still fairly flush from that last frantic field mission up in Nicaragua, old Gaston could spend money as if it were about to go out of style, if he met something pretty to spend it on. And the girls of Costa Rica were as pretty as any in Latin America.

The one he was in bed with now had one hand on the back of his and was rubbing it deeper in her naked lap as she murmured, "Oh, you make me feel so passionate, querido. I confess my dear departed husband never made me feel so, ah, forward. Do you think I am too forward?"

He stopped wondering what the hell Gaston might have wanted with him as he literally grasped what Estralita wanted, and she spread her pale thighs in the moonlight to jerk herself off harder with his willing enough fingers. As he concentrated more politely on pleasing her, she let go of his now nicely moving hand and reached for his semisated shaft to return the favor. She did that great, too.

But as he found himself rising once more to the occasion, they were both still sort of sticky from the last body contact. So he said, "It sure is hot and humid tonight. Let's see if we can't manage a cooler position this time."

Estralita seemed game enough, until she realized what he had in mind as he positioned her across the mattress on her hands and knees and got into position behind her with his bare feet on the floor.

She protested, "Are you mad? Do you expect a woman of my position to make love with an *animal*?"

"Lean back just a little, querida; your position is yummy as hell except for that."

"No, wait, I admit there is more to be said for naked peon lovemaking than my dear departed husband told me, but this is too much to ask of a decent woman and . . . Ay, que linda!"

"I thought you'd like it," said Captain Gringo, grinning down at her pale rump in the moonlight as he proceeded to hump her dog-style, hard. Estralita buried her face in the sheets and protested how humiliated she felt, even as she betrayed how much she liked it by the way she was moving her whole lower body to meet his thrusts. She arched her spine to take it deeper, groaning, "Oh, Madre de Dios, this is fantastico! Not even my dear departed husband ever got it in that deep, querido!"

Captain Gringo growled, "Will you shut up about your dear departed husband and concentrate on the guy you're giving it to *now,* damm it? In the first place, it's not polite to speak ill of the dead, and in the second place I'm not interested in how you learned to screw so good. I just want to screw you good, all right?"

For some reason, that made Estralita laugh like hell, and her laughter did all sorts of interesting things to her warm wet insides. So Captain Gringo started pounding harder, and that must have delighted her even more, because she suddenly gasped, "Oh, Jesus, Maria, y José! I am coming again!"

That made two of them. Captain Gringo clung to her strong hip bones with his hands to keep it all the way in as he fired a nice long burst into her.

Then the door popped open and a strange male voice bellowed, "By the balls of Santiago! What has been going on in here?"

That was a pretty stupid question for anyone to ask a naked man with his dong still in a naked lady, dog-style, but the guy in the doorway was making a stupid move for something under his linen jacket, too. So Captain Gringo popped out of Estralita to pop him with a hard left cross before he could do or say anything else stupid.

The solid punch to the jaw bounced the mysterious intruder's head off the solid wall behind him, damaging him some more before he could manage to sprawl face down and very still at Captain Gringo's bare feet.

The naked American slammed the door shut for privacy before turning to the bare brunette on the bed to ask, "Is this anyone we know?"

Estralita was trying to cover her considerable charms with the end of a sheet as she stared in horror at the stranger Captain Gringo had coldcoked in the moonlight. She gasped. "Do you think he saw what we were doing?"

"Never mind what he saw, damm it! Who the hell *is* he?"

"My husband. Oh, querido, what are we to do?"

Captain Gringo dropped to one knee to feel the side of the unconscious man's neck as he answered, "Damm it, Estralita, you told me the poor bastard was already dead!"

She sobbed. "No, I didn't. Is he dead now?"

"No, thank God, and no thanks to you, you stupid lying bitch! What do you mean, you didn't tell me he was dead? All you've been talking about since you picked me up has been this dear departed husband of yours, goddamm it, and here he is, alive and well, almost!"

She protested, "I did not lie, querido. My dear husband departed over two weeks ago, for to go to Limón on business. He wasn't supposed to be back until the end of the month, and, oh, how shall we ever explain this most distressing business to him when he wakes up?"

Captain Gringo muttered, "Oh boy!" and started scooping up his things. As he dressed, the cheating wife found her underwear, at least, and put it on as she asked again what they were going to tell her husband when and if.

Captain Gringo buckled his shoulder holster, slipped his linen jacket on over it, and picked up his planter's hat, saying, "You'll think of something."

As he headed for the door she wailed, "Wait! You can't leave me here like this for to face the music alone, querido!"

Captain Gringo said, "Sure I can. Just watch my smoke. I don't want to be anywhere near your dear departed husband when he comes back to life a second time on you!"

Captain Gringo had no idea how long it might take to beat the whole story out of the buxom brunette. But he figured he had at least a few minutes' lead on her outraged husband. So he hurried back to the sidewalk cantina to see if Gaston had dropped by yet.

Gaston had. The old Frenchman wasn't there, but he'd left a message of his own. So Captain Gringo grabbed it from the waitress on the fly and whipped around the corner to read it under a side-street streetlamp.

He muttered, "What the hell?" when he got to the part about Gaston meeting him at the American embassy across town. Then he tore up the note and made tracks for his own hotel, resisting the impulse to break into a dead run. For now he was in real trouble. The note had been in Gaston's handwriting, but he was sure the Frenchman would never have written such a dumb suggestion without a gun to his head!

Captain Gringo hadn't always been Captain Gringo. Back in the dear dead days when he'd still thought the world was run on the level, he'd been First Lieutenant Richard Walker of the U.S. Tenth Cavalry. Then Uncle Sam had decided to hang him on a false charge, so he escaped by killing his would-be executioner, and had been running ever since, with a dead-or-alive want chasing him.

Costa Rica was a reasonably safe place for a wanted man.

Or at least it had been before he'd started bouncing Costa Rican husbands off bedroom walls. The local government was easygoing and had no extradition deal with Tio Sam.

But some pricks at the American embassy here in San José had tried once before to grab him and take him back to the States, and they'd almost succeeded, too!

His hotel was around the next corner. He'd whip up to his room and pack a few things before he cut out for . . . where?

It didn't matter. They already had Gaston, and anywhere had to be safer than here right now. He got to the corner and saw that the entrance of his hotel was clear. Then he stopped, whipped back around the corner, and stepped into a dark doorway to light a Havana claro and reconsider his options.

They were all pretty dismal. Gaston could probably hold out longer than a buxom brunette. But if they'd gotten him to write that dumb note, how long could it take them to get a hotel address out of him? The rules of the soldier-of-fortune game were rough. A knockaround guy looked out for his own ass first. Gaston was wanted a lot of places for a lot of things. But not by Uncle Sam. So, yeah, they could let the Frenchman go if he was willing to play ball. Gaston was old enough to be Captain Gringo's father, and he hadn't gotten that old through self-sacrifice. He'd no doubt feel shitty about ratting on a pal. But when push came to shove, it was every man for himself.

The tall American stepped out of the doorway and started walking away from the hotel. The pricks staked out in his room were welcome to the unimportant luggage up there. Captain Gringo had his money and a double-action .38 on him. What more did an ambitious youth need to get ahead in the world?

Where in the world he was headed at the moment was still up for grabs. He couldn't risk the railroad depot.

They probably knew about his occasional redhead and the understanding madam he and Gaston had hidden out with in the past. If they had Gaston, they probably knew every friend the two of them had in San José. So okay, he could just keep walking and be well out of town before sunrise, right?

A big wet toad plopped down on the brim of Captain Gringo's hat. He cursed and kept walking as he braced himself for the inevitable. He'd noticed earlier that the night had been unusually warm and humid. It was cooler now. That meant the sky was about to open up and dump a gully washer any minute now.

Another spoonful-sized warning drop put out his cigar. He grimaced and put the claro away, muttering, "Waste not, want not." He didn't know when he'd next see a tobacco shop with a wooden Indian instead of a cop standing out front. It started to rain harder. Captain Gringo tried to look on the bright side. At least nobody with a lick of sense was going to be out on the streets until the cloud burst let up. He could live with being soaked to the skin, if it improved his chances of living.

He came to the plaza. He ducked into another doorway to scout the situation. The plaza was of course deserted, with the paseo called on account of rain. The cantina across the wide expanse of wet pavement was deserted too. He decided to go around the plaza anyway. He was about to step back out into the rain when a familiar sardonic voice said, "Eh bien, I thought you'd outdistanced me, you species of long-limbed suspicion!"

Captain Gringo turned to stare thoughtfully down at the short damp figure who'd just joined him, asking, "Are you alone, you old goat?"

"Merde alors," Gaston replied. "Do you think anyone

else cares enough about you to get soaked chasing you all over town in a deluge?''

Captain Gringo didn't answer until he'd had a thoughtful look around. Anyone who took Gaston Verrier's word on anything without checking was a chump.

The little Legion deserter didn't look like a sneak. Gaston owed his amazing longevity to the fact that he didn't look like anything in particular. He was one of those gray little guys who could melt into a crowd or a police lineup like he wasn't there. His English was sort of weird, but he could and did pass for a native in Spanish-speaking countries. Women found him reasonably attractive. Most men failed to notice him unless they were bullies who liked to pick on little guys, in which case they were in big trouble.

Gaston had come over with the French Foreign Legion to back the ill-fated play of the so-called Emperor Maximilian in Mexico. When Juarez had started winning with monotonous regularity, Gaston had been pratique, as he put it, about changing sides.

Captain Gringo said, "Speaking of changing sides, what was that shit about meeting you at the American embassy, and how did you get away?"

Gaston said, "I realized later you might have reservations about meeting me there. So I went to your hotel to wait for you. You do stand out on a corner under a streetlamp, even when you are trying not to. So when I regarded your hasty retreat, I most naturally dashed madly after you. Mon Dieu, you do cover ground with those très formidable legs of yours, you damned moose!"

He took Captain Gringo by one elbow as he added, "Meanwhile, it is raining les chats et chiens. Come, we can follow that adorable arcade while staying reasonably dry to a species of café one hopes to be still open, hein?"

Captain Gringo went with him. Anything beat standing in the rain. As they moved along the dark arcade past dark and shuttered shops, he asked the Frenchman to explain the grotesque message, adding, "You know damned well I'm wanted in the States on every charge but the common cold. Did you really think I'd go anywhere near that fucking embassy?"

Gaston said, "I told you I regretted my hasty note, Dick. Voilà, here is the adorable café, and, as you see, we shall have it to our adorable selves as I fill you in on the fantastique deal I made for you, you ungrateful child!"

They went in and took a back booth with their black coffee. Gaston waited until the bored-looking waitress was out of earshot before he explained, "The offer is a thousand a month, U.S. Plus a chance for a full pardon from your President Cleveland if all goes as planned. How do you like the payoff so far?"

The homesick Captain Gringo couldn't believe it. So he didn't. He stared suspiciously across the table at Gaston and said, "Okay, let me fill in the rest. They want me to drop by the embassy like a good little boy and hold out my hands while they slap on the cuffs and tell me all about the neat fair trial I'll get back in the States this time, right?"

"Wrong. I mentioned the time that unpleasant M'sieur Carson tried to trick you back to trip the light fantastique at the end of a rope. They assured me they understand your concern and that there is no need for either of us to contact the U.S. State Department again. In fact, one gets the distinct impression that the deal is to be, how you say, off the books?"

Captain Gringo took another sip of coffee before he said, "Keep talking. I feel better now that I know it's something sneaky."

Gaston uaid, "Eh bien, as you know, your somewhat unpredictable Uncle Sam has been trying to complete the Panama Canal abandoned by the French syndicate that started it. American interests bought out the stock of the bankrupt French. Yankee ingenuity would no doubt make short work of the few modest mountains left between the Atlantic and Pacific, if, alas, the government of Colombia would only be reasonable."

Captain Gringo said, "Get to the damned point. Everyone knows Colombia owns the Isthmus of Panama and isn't about to let anyone else dig another cubic yard of anything, unless they're willing to pay through the nose for the dubious privilege."

Gaston nodded and said, "Exactly. Knowing a formidable amount of lives and money have already been invested in the stalled project, the junta in Bogotá continues to make impossible demands. Meanwhile, there are many ways to deprive a chat of its adorable skin, non?"

Captain Gringo grimaced and said, "Oh, shit, I hope you're not talking about another half-ass funded revolution down that way, pal. When we fought for the old Balboa Brigade that time, we learned the hard way that Colombia has a pretty good army, remember?"

Gaston nodded and replied, "With pain and sorrow. But as you just pointed out, those rebels had half an ass. Forget the lost cause of the unfortunate Balboa Brigade. The new unit we'll be working for is funded indeed, and already set up and dug in."

"Why do they need us, then?"

"As training officers, of course. Money, supplies, and très moderne weapons are already pouring in. The problem is that the rebels backed by Washington and Wall Street, if there is any difference, do not know as much as they should about machine guns, breech-loading field guns, and so forth. That is where you and I come in."

Captain Gringo frowned throughtfully and asked, "Why? Has West Point gone out of business? It seems to me that if I were running things back home I'd send in some regular army guys before I'd hire a guy wanted for murder and desertion!"

Gaston chuckled dryly and replied, "That is no doubt why you are not running things back home, my idealistic youth. I just told you the whole operation is unofficial and burn-before-reading. It would be an act of war to send anyone on the U.S. payroll to help overthrow an established and nominally friendly government, non?"

Captain Gringo shrugged and said, "I said I believed the sneaky part. Okay. When do we leave for where?"

Gaston looked surprised and asked, "Merde alors, just like that, sans the usual tedious argument? Eh bien, our discreet coastal schooner will be waiting for us in Limón. It will put in with us and more ammo at Laguna Chiriquí, weather and Colombian gunboats permitting."

Captain Gringo finished his coffee, put down the cup, and said, "Let's move it out, then. We can still make the night train to Limón if we hurry."

Gaston grinned and said, "I must be improving with age. I expected to have to drag you kicking and screaming all the way. What did it, the offer of a possible pardon?"

Captain Gringo snorted in disgust and said, "I'll believe that when the tooth fairy leaves a dime under my pillow. There's something fishy as hell about the whole deal, and you'd never get me anywhere near Panama again if it was still safe to stay here in Costa Rica."

As they left together Gaston asked, "What am I missing, Dick? Who could be after us here in Costa Rica?"

Captain Gringo said, "There's nobody after you. The poor

slob is after me. I don't want to talk about it. When a guy acts as dumb as I did tonight, he deserves to go to hell. But Panama is closer and it might not be much worse.''

When they got off the train in Limón at dawn, the lowland seaport was wrapped in fog as thick and warm as pea soup. Gaston said he'd been told they would be contacted and given further instructions at the Hotel Alhambra by someone from the quasi-official outfit they'd be working for. Gaston had no idea who or when, so the two soldiers of fortune checked in and took adjoining rooms. Anyone who'd just ridden the night train from San José down the endless hairpin curves of the Sierra Oriental on a hardwood coach seat could do with a hot tub soak and an hour or so stretched out on a soft mattress. The people who were looking for them knew where to find them.

Captain Gringo undressed alone in his own hotel room and draped his still-damp clothes over a couple of chairs under the ceiling fan hopefully to dry a bit. He naturally took his wallet, shoulder rig, and other valuables into the bathroom with him. He'd noticed that the lock between him and the hall was pretty primitive. But he doubted if anyone would steal a straw planter's hat, or damp linen that probably wouldn't fit many natives, in such a classy hotel.

He locked the bathroom door and ran a hot tub as he used the flush commode. The sanitary facilities on the night train had been pretty rough, too.

He got into the tub, lathered himself with a bar of hotel soap that was almost hard enough to use as one of the white bathroom tiles, and lay back to soak. It felt good. At least they hadn't stinted on the hot water. He'd soaked about half an hour and was considering whether to get out or run some more hot water when he heard something sneaky going on in the room outside. He hadn't booked a double room, and Gaston knew enough to knock discreetly before he popped in on a guy with a gun.

The tall American froze in the tub as he strained his ears. He heard it again. It sounded like the rustle of dry silk. His own clothes out there were damp linen, and hardly apt to wander around with nobody inside them in any case.

Captain Gringo slowly got out of the tub, careful not to splash or slosh. Whoever was tossing his room might not know he'd been bathing instead of out. He slid his .38 from the shoulder holster he'd hung near the tub. Then, naked and still wet, he popped out of the john, armed and dangerous.

As he moved in on the figure near the brass bedstead he saw at a glance that the hall door was shut and that the intruder was a dame in a tan pongee dress with her back to him. Or at least she had had her back to him as she'd been opening a drawer of the bed table; then she stiffened and half-turned toward him as he charged.

Her ears and the little nickel-plated whore pistol in her right hand were too slow for Captain Gringo. He dove at her in a flying tackle and disarmed her with his free hand as they fell together across the bed. They bounced like hell with her on the bottom until the springs recovered from the surprise. She looked pretty surprised too as she stared up at him in terror. He had her pinned with his dripping upper torso crushed against her well-filled pongee bodice and one wet thigh between her own. His naked flesh could feel, through her now-damp pongee, that whoever she was she didn't wear anything under her tropic dress. As she struggled weakly under him, her nicely put together curves felt yummy. Her face wasn't bad, either. She was a dishwater blonde of about twenty-five. Her frightened eyes were pale gray. She wore no makeup. So her lips were pale as she pleaded, "Don't hurt me! I'll do anything you say!"

He grinned down at her and said, "You're so right. Just lay still and let me sort out the security situation here. Okay, your gun's on the far side of the bed on the rug. I don't think I need this gun. So we'll just toss it to the foot of the bed for now."

He started patting her down for other hardware with the hand he'd just freed for action. She gasped and protested, "That's my breast you have your hand on, sir!"

He said, "I noticed. It feels like a dangerous weapon indeed, but I don't see how I can take it off you, so what the hell."

He shifted his weight and ran his hand down her now-damp torso to find, as he'd suspected, that she wasn't even wearing a corset. When he got to the really interesting parts, she stiffened, bit her lower lip, and said, "All right. But please don't hurt me!"

He hadn't been thinking of raping her. He'd only wanted to make sure she wasn't one of those sneaky dames who packed a rod between her thighs in one of those tricky garter holsters. On the other hand, if she was offering, he didn't want her to think he was a sissy. So he proceeded to pull her thin pongee skirt up between them as he felt himself rising to the occasion.

She felt what was coming to life against her now-naked thigh, too, and gasped as she said, "Oh, my God, they told me you were a big man, but please be gentle, Captain Gringo!"

So he was. He wedged her thighs apart with his own legs and slid the turgid tip of his old organ grinder up and down the slit between her trembling limbs to lubricate them both before he slowly shoved it in. She hissed in mingled pleasure and dismay until it was all the way in her. Then she relaxed and surrendered completely, saying, "You won't hurt me, *after*, will you?"

As he screwed her at a polite conversational pace to let her get used to the idea, Captain Gringo said, "Let's talk about that. You know who I am. So you have the advantage on me, ma'am."

She giggled despite her anxiety and replied, "I'm Alice Redford, British Intelligence. I swear I meant you no harm."

"Right. That nickel-plated .32 was a present you were sent to slip under my pillow. What the fuck do you Brits have to do with me now? I told your cheap boss, Greystoke, that I didn't want to work for you lime juicers anymore. Every time I have, I've been shortchanged."

She spread her legs wider and began to respond to his slow thrusts with sensuous movements of her own as she murmured, "Could we talk about it after we climax, sir? I confess I'm beginning to enjoy what you're doing to me too much to be interrogated in depth and . . . speaking of depth . . ."

He laughed and said, "Yeah, let's do this right."

She was willing. She helped as he unbuttoned her and slipped the dress up over her head without dismounting. He told her to lock her legs around him, and when she did he moved farther up on the bed with her and slid a pillow under her now most cooperative derriere. Then, as she wrapped her arms as well around his naked body, they kissed for the first time and proceeded to do it right until they'd shared a long protracted orgasm.

As he stopped to get his second wind, Alice throbbed warmly on his soaking shaft as she sighed and said, "Oh, that was lovely. You're right about British Intelligence not paying very well. But this was an unexpected bonus indeed! Could we do it again, darling?"

He said, "In a minute. Before I call anyone *darling* we'd better take advantage of this moment of sanity to learn more about you. What were you looking for just now?"

She moved her hips teasingly and said, "Not this. But I'm so glad I found it."

"I am, too. But cut the bullshit, doll. You were tossing my room when I came out to make friends with you. What were you expecting to find?"

She shrugged, moving her nipples nicely against his bare chest, and said, "Anything interesting, of course. There's no sense in pretending we don't know about you signing up with Los Jurados. But Her Majesty's Service likes to gather all the details, and frankly we're confused about you Yanks. I see you have nothing on paper that would be any use to us. If I could, ah, make it worth your while, could you fill me in a bit on this rather grotesque power play?"

Captain Gringo had already found out something he hadn't known before. Up to now, nobody had mentioned the name of the rebel faction they were supposed to be joining. So, to keep her talking as well as slowly screwing, he said. "What you're giving me is worth my while indeed, doll box. But you didn't find much because I honestly don't know much. Since you know who I am and where I'm going, I'm not giving much away when I tell you that's about as much as I know about the job, so far. To tell the truth, you seem to know all the angles. So how come the rebels call themselves a jury and how come my old pal Greystoke thinks they're grotesque?"

She replied, "Unless Whitehall's missing something, Washington's plan is utterly stupid. You're never going to overthrow the Colombian junta with a ragtag band of guerrilla fanatics. We've offered to back you Yanks when and if your silly President Cleveland stops playing games and simply sends in the gunboats and marines. Great Britain wants the Panama Canal completed as much or more than you do. We have a bigger navy and merchant fleet and it's a bother going all the way around Cape Horn."

Then she dug her nails into his bare buttocks and moaned. "I wish you'd stop teasing me with your own naughty horn and excavate my canal in earnest, damm it!"

He chuckled and started moving faster. But apparently it wasn't fast enough. She pleaded, "Let me get on top. You're driving me crazy, sliding all that lovely stuff in and out so casually!"

He grinned, rolled off, and stretched out on his back for her, as he casually shoved the .38 off the foot of the bed. Alice rolled atop him, settled on his shaft again, and murmured, "Oh, it feels even more so, this way. Did you really think I'd try to shoot you with your own gun, darling?"

He said, "Since you can't, now, let's not worry about it."

So they didn't. The pale blonde leaned forward to brace her upper weight with two soft palms flat against his chest and her firm milky breasts squeezed between her soft upper arms as she got her nether regions in a very interesting position, with her high-button shoes flat on the mattress on either side of his hips so she could move on his erection like a sex-mad cossack dancer.

He would have closed his eyes in pleasure if he really trusted her. As it was, the view was inspiring him to new heights as she slid her velvet lining rapidly up and down. He could tell she'd taken dancing lessons at some time in her shady past, for her legs had to be powerful as well as shapely to sustain the delightful effort. As it was, she began to sweat despite the pleasant draft from the overhead fan before she managed to satisfy herself. When she did begin to climax, she couldn't keep going and feel weakly down against him, moving awkwardly with it only half in her as she sobbed and said, "Oh, Christ, I'm right on the very edge and I can't get over it!"

He knew exactly how she felt. So he rolled her over on her back, hooked an elbow under each of her upraised knees, and long dicked her to glory with his own arms locked in a push-up position, while she came again and again around his plunging manhood. She was pleading for mercy when he satisfied himself as well and collapsed atop her, kissing her passionately for being such a good little girl. When they came up for air, Alice murmured, "I think you've ruined me for life, and I'm ever so grateful to British Intelligence! My God, to think I might have missed out on that if you hadn't caught me being naughty, you naughty boy!"

He chuckled and said, "I'm starting to admire the Union Jack, too. I don't know where in the hell Greystoke recruits you nubile operators. But he sure picks great lays. Did you have to show him how good you were in the hay before he sent you out to spy on people, Alice?"

She pouted her lush lower lip and said, "Don't be beastly. This is the first time I've been required to do this on Her Majesty's service."

He said, "You sure do it great, for a beginner. I'm still hot."

She pulsated teasingly on his semierection and said with a sigh, "So I notice. But I really must be getting back to the embassy, dear. Ah, you do intend to let me leave here alive, don't you?"

He laughed and said, "Not yet," as he began to move in her again.

She protested, "No, really, darling, I have to report back before they begin to worry about me. They warned me you were dangerous and told me to be very very careful. If I don't return soon, they'll think something happened to me and...Oh, Lord, something *is* happening to me again! But hurry, hurry—I really have to get dressed and out of here before all sorts of people come bursting in to rescue me!"

That sounded reasonable. So he rolled her over on her hands and knees to hump her that way, knowing it was the quickest way to come. The pale blonde buried her face in the bedding, moaning with pure animal pleasure as she thrust her white rump invitingly up for his and her pleasure. But as usual, the third time took a little longer, for him, at least. She came ahead of him, or said she had, and relaxed to let him finish. He kept moving, but as long as she seemed calm enough to carry on a sensible conversation now, he told her, "Okay. Here's the deal. You go back to your outfit, tell 'em you got away with tossing my room but didn't find anything. Tell 'em you're going to try and get the info out of me the usual seductive way, and if we play it right we can have a nice dinner on British Intelligence before we do this some more this evening, right?"

She laughed and said, "You're awful. Would you really tell me anything if I seduced you, darling?"

"You already have, so ask away."

"Oh, that feels so nice. But seriously, dear, didn't they tell you *anything* about the mission you and your French friend are on?"

"Nope. And if they don't tell us more, and flash some front money at us, we ain't on it. I told you I've been stiffed by you Brits after pulling chestnuts out of the fire for Queen Vickie a couple of times. I don't work for free these days."

"Ooh, I like the way you're working on *me*! Do you know if the people sending you to help Los Jurados are U.S. government or some sort of semiprivate agency?"

Since he didn't know, there was no sense holding out on

her about it. He said, "It could be either. Both Uncle Sam and the big shots with private capital invested in the stalled canal project must be pretty fed up with the Colombian junta by now. Frankly, I don't care, as long as their money was minted by Uncle Sam. If it's not, the deal's off. So what else can I tell you?"

Alice didn't answer. She sobbed in orgasm and fell forward to lie flat across the bed, groaning and chewing the sheeting as he followed her down and tried to keep it in. He was right on the verge of coming himself when her contractions popped the head out like a slippery melon seed. He reached down, grasped his trembling shaft, and thrust in hard to keep from wasting it on empty air. As her tight warmth clamped down around it again, he exploded inside her at the end of the first deep thrust. Then he realized where he'd come and murmured, "Oops, sorry. Am I hurting you, honey?"

She arched her spine cooperatively to take it a bit more comfortably as she replied, "It doesn't hurt that way once it's all the way in. But do you really have to bugger me, too? Haven't you had enough yet?"

He said, "No." But slowly drew it out of her tight anal opening and rolled away to wipe himself clean as she sat up, smiling at him, and said, "I'll try to get back tonight, if you promise to keep that big thing out of my poor arse, you brute. But now that we've finished coming for now, I really have to go. Ah, could I have my gun back, dear?"

"I guess so. After I take the bullets out of it."

Captain Gringo took another bath after the pale blonde dressed and left. The unexpected pleasure of her company had done more to take the travel kinks out of him than a mere nap would, now. So, finding that his clothes were dry again, he put them on. He'd just finished dressing and was lighting a smoke when Gaston knocked to be let in.

The Frechman sniffed and said, "How odd. There is a distinct scent of perfume and pussy in here, Dick."

Captain Gringo said, "I'll tell you about that after you tell me what's up."

So Gaston said, "Nothing is up. I find that très curious too. It is getting late, and so far nobody has contacted us. I am sure they said the Hotel Alhambra. But it is still très foggy outside and we did arrive at an ungodly hour. Do you suppose nobody knows we've arrived?"

The tall American said, "Somebody knows we've arrived. Let's go down and wait in the hotel bar. American spies may not be as good at reading hotel registers as other spies. I'll tell you about my new perfume on the way."

He filled Gaston in on his visitor as they took the stairs down to the lobby and entered the dark, discreet, and nearly deserted bar room. They took a booth where they could be spotted by anyone with sense enough to look for them but that was private enough to talk.

Gaston waited until their drinks had been served and it was safe to discuss mystery blondes before he observed with one eyebrow raised, "I smell something très fishy about this species of Alice, Dick, and I am not referring to her cunt! Why would the British send spies to find out what their friends in Washington are up to regarding the Panama Canal project? Whitehall and Washington have been working together to see the damned ditch dug. I know our old friend Greystoke is a species of rosey bastard, but this makes no sense. As a Frenchman, I have never understood it, but it remains a simple fact of life that once you strange Americans won your revolution to be free of the British, you turned right around and proceeded to kiss the British ass, non?''

"Well, that may be putting it a little strongly. Mother country and all that rot, I suppose.''

"Merde alors, anyone who treated their mother like you Americans treat the British would be arrested for incest, Dick! Sometimes I feel you crazy Yankees admire the British government more than the British do! Regard how your countrymen reacted to that visit from the Prince of Wales, hein? In London His fat Highness is considered a dull-witted bore who drinks like a fish, eats like a pig, and seduces other men's wives with a lack of discretion that would get anyone but a crown prince killed! Yet, whenever he deigns to visit your proud independent republic, you fall all over one another in adoration of the fat moron!''

Captain Gringo sipped his highball before he replied, "You've made your point. But it's not important. The blonde wasn't working for British Intelligence.''

Gaston blinked and said, "But you just told me she confessed to you she was a British spy, non?''

The tall American shrugged and said, "She had to say *something* when I got the drop on her. She probably heard about the Prince of Wales shaking hands with Buffalo Bill, too.''

Gaston nodded knowingly and said, "Ah, the plot thickens. Since she knew who you were, she knew we've worked with Greystoke and company in the past and probably would not swat a British agent without discussing the matter calmly, hein?''

"That's about the size of it. She slipped up when she said she was working out of the British embassy here in Limón."

Gaston frowned and said, "There is no British embassy here in Limón. Only a consulate, over by the plaza.''

The tall American nodded and said, "That's what I just told you. She'd have known that, had she really been sent by Greystoke. But what the hell, she was making up her cover story on the fly."

Gaston laughed and asked, "Don't you mean on the bed? Eh bien, she could not have been working for your American secret service. She was not from British Intelligence. How do you feel about that très fatigue young Kaiser Willy, Dick? Germany is one of the few maritime nations I can think of who would not wish the canal built."

Captain Gringo shook his head and said, "She was blond enough to be German despite her Mayfair accent. But I dunno, the Germans train their spies pretty good, and she was strictly bush league. She tossed my room without checking to make sure I was out. She didn't really know what the hell she was looking for. And when I caught her she took a pretty Latin way out. Somebody raised her never to argue with a guy who managed to catch her without a chaperon. And she knew this outfit we're mixed up with by its local Hispanic title, too."

Gaston nodded and said, "Colombian. They grow plenty of blondes up in Bogotá. But does that not mean the government we are out to overthrow is already onto us, Dick?"

Captain Gringo took another sip of gin and tonic and said, "Sure. So what? If the rebel faction is already holding part of the Isthmus of Panama, Colombia would have to have noticed by this time. You and I are known soldiers of fortune. Soldiers of fortune go where there's a war or revolution going on. Even a bush-league intelligence outfit could add *those* figures up! The only question before the house now is do we hang around here until somebody contacts or shoots us, or do we quit while we're ahead?"

"I thought you couldn't go back to San José, Dick?"

"I probably shouldn't, for a while. But now that I've had time to reconsider, there are lots of places that have to be safer than Panama."

He took out his pocket watch and added, "Let's give it until siesta time. That's the best time to move down here if we decide to make it bye-bye. It gives them all the fucking time anybody sensible could ask for, as well."

"What about your date this evening with adorable Alice?"

"I lied. There's no way I can take the bullets out of her gun before I meet her, and dumb spies make me nervous."

As if the remark about dump spies had been an entrance cue, a lean, hungry-looking guy in a loose-fitting Panama suit came in to join them without being invited and said, with a midwestern American accent, "I'm Bowman. My friends call me Jim. But you two can call me Mr. Bowman."

Captain Gringo muttered, "Up yours, too." But Gaston smiled politely and asked, "To what do we owe this pleasure, M'sieur Bowman?"

The other American said, "It's not pleasure. It's strictly business. I was against hiring either of you, but who listens? So, okay, here's the deal. There's a schooner down the quay. Steam aux, black sails, named the *Nombre Nada*. The skipper's somebody I wouldn't trust as far as I could toss her whole fucking boat, but ours is not to reason why. They want you guys aboard her. But you'd better wait until the siesta starts, so all the greasers will be beddy-bye when you board. Got it?"

Bowman started to rise. Captain Gringo snapped, "Sit down, Bowman. You haven't finished telling us who *they* might be. We haven't seen any money, either."

The sarcastic Bowman said, "Never mind who they might be. Suffice it to say they've hired you to help some other thugs set up a Panamanian republic. Do it right and you know about the possible pardon, even if you don't deserve one as a murderer and renegade. You'll be paid your first advance when you're on the high seas, aboard the gunrunning tub. Any other dumb questions?"

Captain Gringo said, "Yeah. How would you like to take a flying fuck at a rolling doughnut? The deal is off unless and until I see some front money, friend!"

Bowman frowned and said, "I don't have any money on me, damm it."

"So go and *get* it, then. But make it snappy. You're so right about la siesta being a good time to cover ground without too many people noticing. You've got, oh, about twenty minutes."

The contact man didn't move. He said, "I wouldn't try to pull out this late in the game if I were you, Walker. The local cops don't knock off for siesta and you two guys are wanted lots of places for lots of things, you know."

Then he froze and turned rather pale as he found himself staring down the muzzle of Captain Gringo's .38. The tall American smiled pleasantly and asked, "Would you like to rephrase that last remark, friend?"

Bowman licked his lips and said, "Oh, hell, everybody knows the Costa Rican cops don't bother guys who haven't done anything in Costa Rica."

Captain Gringo nodded and said, "You've got less than twenty minutes now. In case we don't see you again, adiós, motherfucker."

Bowman rose with a muttered curse and left, walking fast. Captain Gringo put the gun away with a dry chuckle and said, "I think we're about to see some front money."

Gaston said, "He did seem in a hurry. Why didn't we want him to know we know the *Nombre Nada* and its formidable female captain, Esperanza, Dick?"

Captain Gringo shrugged and replied, "Why tell anything to a guy who won't tell *us* anything?"

"True, but if Esperanza has agreed to run the guns and supplies, the deal already commences to smell better, non? We both know your big Basque amazon is too wise in the ways of the world to mix her adorable boat and body up in anything distinctly off-color. If she and her cut-throat crew have agreed to run guns to the rebels, it is a safe bet she has checked out the rather unpleasant people we seem to be working for."

Captain Gringo said, "We're not working for anyone yet. If I know Esperanza, she already has her own front money. That's why I called his bluff. I wouldn't want her to think I'm getting soft in my old age."

Gaston chuckled and said, "I doubt she'll leave you soft very long, once she has you aboard her boat and herself, hein. Ah, to be young and adored by big Basque brunettes. I wonder if she'll have a friend for me this time."

Captain Gringo consulted his watch again without answering. He was sort of looking forward to another pleasure cruise and with one of the few old gal pals he could trust not to try to trap him either into wedding bells or jail. But business came before pleasure and he meant what he'd told the surly Bowman.

He looked around for someone to serve him another highball. Their waiter had wandered off somewhere. He picked up his empty and Gaston's almost empty glass and moved over to the bar for a refill. As he moved back to the table, the waiter came out from the back and shot him a dirty look. He sat down again, muttering, "There goes half his tip. I'm sure getting sick of meeting unpleasant people in this fucking town."

Gaston said, "It must be the humidity. It is still foggy out, but now that the sun is near the zenith it feels more like a steambath than your usual fog, non?"

"Drink up. We're getting out of here one damned way or the other, poco tiempo."

Bowman almost didn't make it. The two soldiers of fortune had paid their tab and Captain Gringo was figuring the proper tip for a sullen waiter when the sullen American came in, sweating like a man who'd just run some through a steambath.

He handed Captain Gringo a fat envelope, saying, "It's all there. They didn't like it much. So you guys had better be as good as some say you are."

Captain Gringo opened the envelope and began to count the soggy bills. Bowman said, "Damm it, Walker, I told you it was all there, and you have to get aboard that fucking schooner on the double. They'll be weighing anchor anytime now."

Captain Gringo didn't answer until he'd counted it all, handed half to Gaston, and headed for the door, saying, "Okay. We know the *Nombre Nada*. It's been nice talking to you, prick."

Bowman tagged along, saying, "Not so fast. I'm boarding the schooner with you."

Captain Gringo muttered, "Oh, shit," and Gaston said, "Merde alors," which meant the same thing. Bowman explained, "I'm acting as the liaison officer between, ah, us and El Criado Publico. You may as well know I've got orders to keep an eye on you two as well."

"I never would have guessed," Captain Gringo said dryly.

It wasn't dry outside. The steamy fog was thick as hell and the pavement under them glistened wetly as they moved over to the waterfront.

What they could see of the cobblestone quay was deserted because of la siesta. Bowman peered through the fog to get his bearings and said, "This way. The *Nombre Nada*'s about two city blocks down the quay."

One couldn't have proven it by either soldier of fortune as they followed him. There was just enough visibility to keep from walking off the edge of the seawall, and from time to time they passed dark ghostly shapes that could have been moored sailing vessels or tall pines rooted in the fetid salt water of the harbor, for all one could really see of them. Bowman pointed at nothing much but a fuzzy double blotch in the fog ahead and said, "There she is," just as all hell broke loose.

There were eight or a dozen in the gang. It was hard to tell as they closed in from all sides in the swirling fog. They were armed with knives and clubs. One in the lead made the natural mistake of assuming Gaston was the easy target of the three. So Gaston drew first blood by kicking higher than most cancan dancers could have and removed the thug's nose with the heel of his mosquito boot.

As the mutilated attacker did an unconscious backflip one way, the wiry little Frenchman cartwheeled the other on one hand, drawing his double-edged dagger with his free hand from its sheath under the back of his collar, to land ten yards away in a knife fighter's crouch. Since he found himself facing a startled knife fighter, Gaston knifed *him*.

The two who'd closed in on Captain Gringo from either side were surprised too, when their intended victim moved with astounding speed for a man his size, grabbed each by the nape of the neck, and crashed their heads together like a cymbal player going for the crescendo of the "1812 Overture." The resultant sound was more a loud wet crunch than what he might have managed with brass instead of bone. But when he let go and spun away, they both hit the damp cobblestone pavement and just stayed there, limp as rag dolls with the stuffing knocked out of them.

Captain Gringo had spun away because a third attacker had thrown a barrel stave end over end through the space where his head had just been. He saw two others had Bowman by each arm and were trying either to pull him down or to split him like a wishbone. Captain Gringo charged in before they could do either, and when he decked the one holding Bowman's right arm, the one who'd been tugging on the left let go and tried to get away. He might have, had Bowman not swung his freed right fist and caught him at the base of the skull, dropping him like a poleaxed steer.

Then Bowman went down like another poleaxed steer when somebody deeper back in the fog nailed him with a lucky cobblestone. Bowman's fall was cushioned when he flopped face down across his own victim, bleeding at the hairline.

A length of two-by-four whirled at Captain Gringo, but missed when the soldier of fortune crabbed to one side, into the path of another barrel stave coming at him end over end! He blocked it with his left elbow. It hurt like hell when it bounced off his funny bone. But the guy who really got hurt was the thug who'd thrown it. He was still staring at Captain Gringo when Gaston danced up behind him to plant a boot heel deep in his right kidney.

After that the party started getting rougher.

A sore loser between Captain Gringo and the seawall pegged a shot at him with an old single-action cap-and-ball conversion. He learned the hard way never to miss with one's first shot when firing antiques at serious people. Captain Gringo whipped out his own gun and blew him off the quay into the fetid harbor water before he could recock and aim.

Another gun went off, giving away its owner's position in

the fog with its dull orange muzzle flash. So Captain Gringo fired back at it, and was still crabbing away from his own muzzle flash when he heard the satisfying sound of metal clanking on cobblestone.

Gaston laughed boyishly and shouted, "Eh bien, I too shall take the gloves off, hein?"

What he really meant was that he was tired of fooling around. He drew his own .38 and proceeded to spray bullets into the swirling fog as Captain Gringo reached down, grabbed the unconscious Bowman by the right wrist with his own left hand, and shouted, "Cover me! I'll drag him to the schooner!"

He did. It was rough on Bowman's linen suit and he'd never see his hat again, but by the time they were close enough to the *Nombre Nada* to make out the gangplank, the gang that had attacked them had faded back into the fog to reconsider their options.

As Captain Gringo keel hauled Bowman up the gangplank, a wary voice on board called out, "Parar! Quien es?"

The voice was female, albiet deep-throated, so Captain Gringo called back, "Hold your fire, Esperanza. It's me, Dick Walker!"

His challenger gave a delighted girlish squeal and moved down the gangplank to meet him. The gangplank sagged alarmingly. For aside from the combined weight of Captain Gringo, Bowman, and Gaston, Esperanza was one big dame.

The buxom Basque brunette wasn't fat. Esperanza led too active a life to accumulate much useless lard. But her figure was full and Junoesque, despite being mostly muscle, and Esperanza stood about six feet tall in her rope-soled sandals. As usual, the lady gunrunner was dressed to command a seagoing vessel, not to flirt. So she had on white duck seaman's culottes instead of a skirt, and her full-breasted upper torso was covered, but hardly hidden, by a striped Basque sailor shirt a couple of sizes too small. Her long black hair was bound under a red piratical bandanna. Her big gold earrings were either Esperanza's only concession to feminity or an attempt to convey further ferocity.

Captain Gringo laughed at her and said, "You look like a sissy pirate."

Esperanza enveloped him in a bear-hug and replied, "You look like a sight for sore eyes, querido! I was hoping it would be you when they told me they'd hired a big Americano gun. Now I see I did not burn all those candles in vain. What happened to that unpleasant gringo you are feeling me up with? We just heard shots."

Captain Gringo removed Bowman's limp hand from Esperanza's crotch as she let go of him and said, "Let's get him on board and cast off poco tiempo. You heard shots aimed at us, and they may come back for the rematch!"

Esperanza nodded, turned, and led them all aboard, shouting orders to her crew through the fog in a foghorn voice. So, by the time they had the unconscious Bowman stretched out on a bunk in the cabin already assigned to him, the *Nombre Nada* was backing away from the Limón waterfront with her reversed auxiliary screw. Esperanza told her Chinese cook and/or ship's surgeon to do something about the nasty cut on the liaison officer's head, then led Captain Gringo and Gaston back out on deck. She glanced up at the sails flopping limply in the fog above them and called out to the invisible helmsman, ordering him to steer for the harbor entrance under power against the trades and then tack south-sou'east until further notice.

She waited until they felt the screw reverse under the stern before she nodded in satisfaction and said, "Well, I suppose you muchachos wish for to see what I'm delivering this trip to El Criado Publico, no?"

They agreed and she led them to a hatchway leading down to the hold. She flipped a switch and turned on her new Edison illumination, asking, "How do you like the way we've modernized since you were last aboard?"

Captain Gringo said, "Nice. I noticed your engine sounds more serious than before, Esperanza."

She laughed and said, "I owe that to you, querido mio. Thanks to my loaning la *Nombre Nada* to British Intelligence that time, the old tub will never be the same. Before they got her back to me they fitted her with an electric generator as well as new internal organs. Same old hull and sails, but now I have a big steam screw that can outrun damned near anything but a torpedo ram."

Then she nudged Captain Gringo and added, with a girlish giggle, "Of course, if your ram is still out to catch my screw..." Then she remembered Gaston was right behind them and blushed modestly.

Captain Gringo chuckled and said, "Let's talk about the way this El Criado Publico is hung. What do you know about him and his jurado whatevers, by the way?"

Esperanza led them deeper into the hold, switched on another overhead bulb, and said, "See the cargo for yourselves. I don't know anything about the rebel faction Tio Sam seems so fond of, muchachos. I have never heard of los jurados and their Great Public Servant before, and I thought I knew everyone in the revolution game down Panama way.

They say El Criado Publico is a pure Spanish blanco. A law professor before he went loco, I think."

Captain Gringo pried open a case as Gaston asked Esperanza why she thought the leader of the faction they'd been sent to help was crazy. The female gunrunner shrugged and said, "He has to be, if he thinks he can beat the Colombian army and navy. They are sons of the bitch, but good. I have played tag along the Mosquito Coast with Colombian gunboats in the past, as you know. That is why I am charging double for this run."

Captain Gringo checked the action of the Maxim machine gun in the crate marked "Farm Implements." The machine gun was factory new, and for once packed right, in petroleum jelly. It was chambered for the same .30-30 rounds most military rifles fired down here. But he'd had grim experience in the past with some .30-30 ammo. So he opened a case of the same as Gaston asked Esperanza more about the size and condition of the rebel army they were bound to join.

Esperanza shrugged and replied, "Really, Gaston, you are asking the wrong person about such matters. I only run guns to rebels. I'm not dumb enough to *join* them!

"But you have put into Laguna Chiriquí before, non?"

"Of course. This will be my sixth run. The lagoon is big and mostly surrounded by mangrove swamps. The place we are making for is a native fishing village, dominated by an old fort left over from the Spanish colonial era. El Criado Publico is using that as his headquarters. I haven't been inside the walls even one time. We drop off the ammo and supplies at one pier running out to modest depth. Rebel porters take over from there. I've let some of my crew go ashore for to get laid in the village. Myself, I stay aboard. I can't even tell you how many fighting men los jurados have, Gaston. Everyone

I've seen, at a distance, just looked to me like the usual pobrecitos."

Captain Gringo found the machine-gun ammo to be not only the right bore but well seated in new canvas machine-gun belts. He shut the lid with a satisfied nod and asked Esperanza if she had a record of just how many rifles she'd delivered so far.

The big brunette answered, "Records? For why would I keep records, querido? I am paid for the run, not the stupid shit I deliver. Each time they give me a bill of lading for to give the rebels along with the cargo when I get through the blockade. Since I seldom throw cargo overboard, there has been no unkind discussion about the tally up to now."

"The rebel officers accepting delivery keep the bills of lading?"

"Of course. What would *I* do with them? I am too delicate for to wipe my ass with heavy bond paper. What makes you two so interested in exact numbers?"

Captain Gringo pried open another crate as Gaston explained how, if they knew how many rifles the rebels had, they'd have some idea of très important numbers indeed, adding, "When Dick and I fought for the late lamented Balboa Brigade down in Panama, the Colombians sent a full regiment in to mop us up, including a heavy-weapons company."

Captain Gringo moved some of the wood shavings in the crate out of the way and said, "Here's something in your department, Gaston. Four-pound artillery rounds. You like?"

"Only if I am not required to toss them by hand," sighed Gaston, turning to Esperanza to ask if she remembered delivering any field guns to los jurados in the past.

She thought and asked, "Do you mean cannon? No. Had I had to winch cannon over the side I feel sure I would have noticed. Why?"

Gaston growled, "Merde alors! She asks why! Esperanza, my pet, to fire four-pound cannon rounds one must have a cannon, non? I fail to understand why even a fool would send artillery shells to a rebel army that has no artillery!"

Esperanza shruged and said, "Maybe they already have some cannon in that Spanish fort. Or maybe they'll give me some to deliver next run. I've been making almost one run a week since this busines started. So far, they haven't told me when I'll be making the last one."

Captain Gringo started to ask her more about the mysterious outfit they all seemed to be working for. But just then the schooner caught the trades with her sails and heeled hard to starboard, throwing them all off balance. Esperanza fell back against a wall of crates as Captain Gringo followed, putting out his hands to brace himself and bracing himself indeed on one of the big brunette's tits. She smiled up at him and reeled him in with her own strong arms, thrusting her nicely padded pubic mound against his fly as she laughed and asked, "Oh, is that all for me?"

He laughed back and said, "We seem to be out to sea and on our way. I just felt the screw stop."

Esperanza's voice was throaty and earthy as she answered, "No, you didn't. The screw's just *starting*, querido mio!"

Gaston rose from the chest he'd landed on and murmured, "I'd better see if our friend Bowman is all right. Do you children want me to turn out the light as I leave?"

Since neither could answer while kissing so warmly, Gaston simply left, not bothering with the illumination. So Esperanza's big black eyes were warm and inviting as they came up for air and she started to work on his buttons, saying, "You undress *me*, querido. It's more romantico that way, no?"

He laughed and protested, "Down here in the hold, for chrissake? What's the matter with your stateroom?"

She went on unbuttoning him as she explained, "We'll spend the night in my quarters, of course. But it might be bad for discipline if my crew saw me invite a man there while I'm standing watch."

"You call this standing watch?"

"Sí, we are inspecting the cargo. Don't worry. Nobody else is allowed in the hold without orders."

Being a rather basic businesswoman, Esperanza had worked on his belt and fly buttons first. So as his pants fell around his ankles he returned the favor by unfastening her culottes and letting them fall around hers. She stepped out of them and stood with her long shapely legs apart, bracing her ample derriere against the crates behind her as she took his erection in hand and guided it in for a wall job as he spread his own legs to lower his center of gravity. As he entered her they both hissed in pleasure. But he couldn't help laughing and saying, "Well, hello there. Long time no see!"

She raised her shapely arms above her head as he peeled off the tight striped shirt, adding, "Wow, long time no see those great bazooms of yours, either!"

She started gyrating her skilled, familiar vagina on his old familiar dong while she got rid of his jacket and opened his shirt under the gun rig to pull his bare flesh against her own, crooning, "Oh, it's so nice when old friends get together again. Have you missed me, Deek?"

"What do you think?" he replied, cupping one of her big buttocks in either palm to start thrusting seriously. She moaned in pleasure but answered with a realistic little smile, "You've probably done this to a hundred women since the last time you were in me, no?"

"Well, not a hundred. You seem to have kept in practice too."

She laughed and began to bump harder, contracting skillfully to milk him on the back strokes as she protested, "Only with discreetly met landlubbers, damm it. A sea captain who doesn't believe in fucking the crew doesn't get the opportunities a man in your line of work does. But whoever taught you that nice new angle has my undying gratitude. Ooh, that feels so nice on my clit!"

It must have. The big brunette suddenly groaned as if she'd been stabbed, shuddered in orgasm, and went rubber-limbed on him. He tried to keep her upright, but her smooth buttocks slipped from his now-sweaty grasp and Esperanza slid to the floor facing his frustrated, raging erection. But, as ever, she was a considerate lover, and so as she knelt at his still booted feet she took the matter in hand and sucked it the rest of the way off for him, which left him pretty rubber-kneed, too. Esperanza did everything well indeed.

As they lay side by side on the rough planking of the hold, smiling fondly at each other, Esperanza said, "You were right. We should have gone to my stateroom and the hell with what the crew might have said. It's my ship, and I'm really too weak at heart to make love on my feet."

He moved closer and started massaging her between her big strong thighs as he pointed out, "We're not standing up now."

She said, "Es verdad. But I don't know about these splintery planks, querido mio. I know I'd never be able to stop for a mere splinter or two in my derriere, once we got started. But we're in the tropics and God knows what sort of infection your knees and my bottom might pick up."

He said, "Yeah, we'd better quit while we're ahead. I can hold out until sunset if you can."

She said she didn't know if she could, as he helped her back to her feet. She plastered her naked body against his and said, "Play with me some more down there, por favor. I fell off like a schoolgirl before I finished coming. Perhaps this time if I am resolved to stay the course . . .''

He led her over to a stack of boxes. They were new and, unlike the decking, made of smooth planed pine. He perched her on the pile with her feet off the deck. Then he said, "Lean back. One good turn deserves another, and I'll take your word you haven't been with anyone else since the last time you had a bath.''

She did as she was told, spreading her big thighs in anticipation, but asking, "Are you sure you don't mind? Maybe if we tried to go sixty-nine . . .''

"We'd wind up crippled,'' he replied, dropping into position as he added, "Mutual orgasm is neat, but it won't work in an alley or a cargo hold. Let's try an experiment.''

Esperanza lay flat, moaning and drumming her heels on the boxes on either side of him as he proceeded to tongue her clit and run two stiff fingers in and out of her at the same time. She bunched and unbunched her firm buttocks to literally fuck his face as she pleaded, "More! More!''

So he got three fingers up her and tried for all four as she pulsated on them. But he had big hands, and Esperanza, for all her size, was built smaller than many a petite Latin doll he'd explored in the past. The only place his pinky would fit was up her tight anal opening. So that's where he shoved it.

She gasped, "Oh, you're so wicked, thank God. But don't get ideas. That finger feels just right, but I'd never be able to take the real thing in my little . . . Oh, Jesus, Maria, y José, I'm cominggggg!''

He moved his tongue and fingers faster until she'd enjoyed a long, shuddering orgasm and gone limp as a dishrag again before he rose and thrust his own reinspired shaft into her to finish, legs braced, as he ran it in and out of her soft moist flesh until it exploded inside her.

She sighed dreamily and said, "I felt that. I like to feel so admired. But maybe we had better save some for later tonight, no?"

He chuckled and said, "Yeah, enough of these light lunches. We'll enjoy a full meal and maybe dessert the right way. You do still have that feather mattress in your quarters, right?"

"Jesus, take it out or *move* it, Deek! I don't know why you have such an effect on me, but you know you do."

He pulled her erect, kissed her warmly as he slid out of her, and then they got dressed as if nothing had happened. But as they started to leave the hold, Esperanza said, "Kiss me again and then I'll be good, Deek."

So he did, and she said, "Muchas gracias. It's good to have you aboard again, Deek. If I were the marrying kind, you would never get away from me again, you know."

He said, "Don't talk dirty. One of the things I like best about you is that you play the game like a knockaround gent, Esperanza."

"Oh? Don't you like the ass I give you every time we meet?"

"Yeah, that too. Let's go topside and see how safe both our asses are right now."

As the day wore on, the weather held lousy for sailing but great for gunrunning. The trades were blowing just fresh enough to move the *Nombre Nada* at a modest clip without blowing away the fog. From time to time they'd sail through a clear patch, and with the winds so light, the sunlit patches felt as if someone had suddenly opened a furnace door above them. But then they'd be back in the cooler fog, which would have made Captain Gringo feel a lot better had they been farther off the treacherous Mosquito Coast.

He asked Esperanza about that as they stood together near the taffrail, out of earshot from the impassive Indio at the helm. Esperanza explained that she knew all too well about the coral reefs they were risking her keel on, but added that it was a stout keel and that the gunboats on patrol farther out to sea could really do a lot more damage with their deck guns when you got down to brass tacks. So he said she was the skipper and went to see how Bowman was making out.

He found the liaison officer still unconscious but not alone in his cabin. A little redhead wearing a Gibson Girl blouse and an ankle-length skirt above her high-button buff calf shoes was seated on the bunk beside Bowman, wiping his forehead with a damp towel. She shot Captain Gringo a timid smile as he came in and asked, "Are you the one who saved my Jim from those awful men, sir?"

He said, "I'm Dick Walker. Sometimes a guy needs saving. Who on earth are you, ma'am?"

"Oh, I'm sorry. I'm Martha Pendergast, Jim's intended."

The tall American frowned down at her and demanded, "Intended for what? Didn't Bowman tell you we're on our way to join up with a rebel army?"

"Yes, and isn't it thrilling? You must be the one they call Captain Gringo. Tell me the truth, do you really think I'll get to see any real fighting down in Panama?"

"I sure hope not, ma'am! No offense, but this is really dumb! Nobody said anything to us about girls tagging along. Do the people your Jim is working for know he brought you along?"

The redhead looked bewildered. He was getting the impression that it was easy for her. For, while she was a pretty little thing, she didn't look too bright, and they already knew her boyfriend was pretty stupid. She said defensively, "Jim said it was our own business. I told him I'm his intended. We may be able to marry in Panama. Jim says they have a nice provisional government already set up there, with justices of the peace and everything, see?"

Captain Gringo said, "Honey, I don't know what the rebels have set up. But I know Colombia has a modern army and navy. I know they hold rather draconian views on rebels, too. If you were to fall into their hands, they'd execute you for sure, after."

"After what?"

"Never mind. Move over and let me see if he's ever going to wake up enough for me to tell him what I think of him for bringing you along."

She made room for him to kneel by the bunk and examine the knocked-out Bowman. He had one hell of a bump on his skull, but nothing as solid as bone moved under the flesh when Captain Gringo felt his injury. Martha said, "Careful. Don't hurt poor Jim."

He replied, "Poor Jim's already hurt. I'm trying to figure out how bad. His breathing seems okay. Flesh a little cool, but he's not in real shock. If he comes to and nobody else is around, make sure he doesn't try to leap out of bed at you. Sometimes a guy recovering from concussion feels better than he really is when he wakes up. The tricky part will be to keep him quiet in bed for at least a full twenty-four, no matter what he says he feels like. Got that?"

"I understand. I read some books on first aid when I was young. I was planning, one summer, to be a nurse when I grew up."

He didn't ask her what she now wanted to be when she grew up. He lifted one of Bowman's eyelids and, yeah, it was concussion all right. The guy figured to be out of touch with the world for a few more hours at least. He told the redhead this and got back to his feet. She asked, "Who were those men who attacked poor Jim, Colombian spies?"

He shrugged and said, "It could work more than one way. A waiter I had down as just a sullen dope-off may have overheard us discussing money—lots of money—and done what comes naturally to the underpaid. He ducked out awhile. So he may have told some local thugs about three rich tourists wandering through the fog well heeled."

"Oh, I thought poor Jim was attacked by spies."

"Poor Jim wasn't the only one there. I said it worked more than one way. There's an outside chance they were Colombian agents. They acted more like plain old thugs than paid assassins. But I did brush with a no-kidding spy working for somebody or other, back in Limón."

"Really? Oh, how exciting! What did he look like?"

"Exciting. Try to remember what I said about keeping Bowman in bed, but don't do it the naughty way. It could kill him. I'm going back on deck."

As he left, she asked him what he meant about keeping anyone in bed the naughty way. He didn't answer. She couldn't be *that* dumb, but she was spoken for, and, come to think of it, so was he. He was smiling wryly when he stepped out on deck and met Gaston. The Frenchman said, "I have been up in the bows. They have a baby deck gun left over from the Siege of the Alamo mounted there. What do you think about one of those Maxims in the hold instead, hein?"

Captain Gringo said it was a good idea but that they'd better tell the skipper before they shifted any of her cargo. As they walked aft, Gaston asked, "What are you grinning about now? I observed the redhead traveling with that species of an idiot. But you weren't with her long enough to smile so smugly."

The tall American said, "I'm not smug. I'm chagrined. Have you ever noticed how it never rains but it pours? How many shitty tramp schooners have we voyaged on without one decent lay to be found on board? So, okay, let a guy take a sea voyage with one great lay in sight, and presto, the devil shoves another likely prospect in his face."

Gaston shrugged and said, "I said I saw her. I agree the redhead looks très easy as well as not bad. But if you want to pass on that formidable big Basque femme, I hope you'll remember your *friends*, Dick!"

Captain Gringo chuckled and said, "Down, boy. It wouldn't work if I was willing to fix you up with Esperanza. But feel free about the redhead, if you want to try for it. No use both of us missing out on that."

Gaston sighed and said, "Alas, I fear they both regard me as a father figure, the poor young dears. Esperanza is young enough to be my daughter. Come to think of it, she could be. But the redhead could be my granddaughter, and even dirty old men must draw the line somewhere, non?"

Then he brightened and added, "Perhaps there will be some dirty old *women* where we are going. One of the crewmen told me there is plenty of amour to be found at Laguna Chiriquí. He was bitching that some of it was old and ugly. Laguna Chiriquí sounds like my kind of town."

The sun burst through the overcast as they joined Esperanza once more on the poop. Captain Gringo told her he thought it might be a good idea to mount at least one machine gun fore and aft. Esperanza shook her head and said, "A good idea, querido, but not in my contract. My orders are that nothing leaves the hold until the rebels accept delivery. Perhaps that Bowman could give you permission, since he works for the people who hired us all, no?"

Captain Gringo nodded, said he'd ask, and led Gaston

away before the little Frenchman could say anything. Gaston asked, "How can we get Bowman's permission to even piss in the hold if he is out like the light, hein?"

"Easy. Guys suffering concussion say all sorts of things they might or might not remember later. You get the redhead out of the cabin some damned way and I'll get permission to unlimber some guns from her knocked-out intended, right?"

"Ah, très bien. One forgets how sneaky you have become since you started traveling with a rogue like me."

So they went back to Bowman's cabin, Gaston lured her out on deck so his comrade could examine her intended for possible injuries of an indelicate nature, and a few minutes later Captain Gringo rejoined them to say, "He's only got that bump on the head. I think he's starting to come to. At least he spoke to me just now."

Martha clapped her hands and said, "Oh, keeno! What did he say, Dick?"

"Just a few words about security, before he passed out again. You'd better go back to him and hold his hand. He may wake up again, see?"

She did. So the two soldiers of fortune went down to the hold and brought up a couple of Maxims and enough ammo to matter, making two trips.

They mounted the first on the taffrail, explaining to Esperanza that he'd gotten permission from the semiconscious liaison officer, who apparently outranked them all. The trusting Esperanza didn't question this. As Gaston had explained in the past, Basques never lied to a friend and so couldn't imagine anyone they trusted even telling them a harmless fib.

They were setting up the second machine gun in the bows when the schooner plowed through another fog bank, sailed out the other side, and almost crashed head-on into a bigger gunboat going the other way!

All hell broke loose as everyone on both sides reacted by instinct without time to really think. Esperanza sprang to the helm in the stern of the *Nombre Nada* and swung the wheel hard over as someone on the bridge of the big armor-plated gunboat did the same. The vessels passed at point-blank pistol range. So of course some slobs aboard the gunboat opened up with their small arms. A Colombian ensign fluttered from the jack staff of the gunboat, and, while the *Nombre Nada* flew no flag at all, the patrol-boat crew obviously knew who they were shooting at!

They shot the *Nombre Nada* up indeed, though she was too close in for them to depress their more serious deck guns. Captain Gringo muttered, ''Oh, shit,'' and swung the Maxim muzzle toward the gunboat as Gaston shoved a belt in for him. The excitement had brought a whole mess of Colombian seamen out on deck by now. So when the tall American traversed said deck with a long burst of automatic fire, the results were grim for the Colombian navy.

White-clad figures dropped and either writhed in agony or just lay still on the deck plates under the long line of bare steel spots Captain Gringo drew on the gray armor plate from stem to stern. Then he saw that the bows of the *Nombre Nada* we no longer at the right angle, leaped up, and ran the length of the schooner to man the taffrail gun and fire a long range raking burst into the gunboat as they entered another fog bank.

As they did so, Esperanza shouted, ''Reef all sails!'' and signaled ''full speed ahead'' with her engine-room telegraph as she swung the wheel hard over again.

Captain Gringo said, ''Good thinking. When they get turned around they'll come boiling with a bone in their teeth along your last known course. But how far are we from shore, Esperanza?''

''How the fuck should I know, and who the fuck cares?''

That sounded reasonable enough, when one considered the option of standing out to sea with a deep-draft gunboat in the neighborhood. So as Gaston joined them in the stern, Captain Gringo was putting another belt in the Maxim. The Frenchman cast a thoughtful glance over the rail and muttered, "I hate to be a spoilsport, but I can see sharks as well as adorable coral heads in that shallow water, Esperanza."

Before the big brunette at the helm could answer, the *Nombre Nada* ground to a shuddering stop as her keel cut into chalky coral. Gaston sighed and said, "See what I mean?"

Esperanza said something dreadful in her own private language and signaled reversed engines. As they stared over the stern, the sea churned the color of watered milk, but the *Nombre Nada* didn't move.

A crew member popped his head out a deck hatch and shouted. "We are taking on water, Captain Esperanza!"

Esperanza shouted back, "Don't stand there like an idiot, then. Start the fucking pumps!"

As he dropped out of sight, Esperanza signaled the engine room to stop the useless screw, then turned to stare seaward into the fog, asking quietly, "Does anyone have any suggestions? the *Nombre Nada* and me are both stuck!"

The only thing that was getting better as the day got older was the visibility. The afternoon sun was beginning to burn off the fog at last, but that was no improvement to the people aboard the grounded schooner, with a gunboat patroling somewhere near enough to matter!

Esperanza's almanac said the tide had to ebb farther before it rose again. So as the schooner began to rest even more of her tonnage on her keel, the seam she'd sprung kept leaking more by the minute.

As of the moment, the *Nombre Nada*'s steam-powered bilge pumps were dealing with the leak okay. But to have steam power one had to burn oil, and, while the *Nombre Nada*'s long skinny smokestack wasn't sending up a very big plume, any plume at all could be fatal if an unfriendly lookout spotted it on the rapidly clearing horizon. So Esperanza went below to see about damage control after sending her own lookout up the mainmast.

Because of the increasing heat below decks, most of the others on board had gathered on deck, save for the unhappy engine-room gang and Esperanza's damage-control party. The redhead steering the now more-or-less recovered Jim Bowman by one arm spotted Captain Gringo and Gaston in the stern and led her intended back to them, saying, "I did try to keep him comfy in bed, but it was so hot in there."

Bowman blinked owlishly at the soldiers of fortune and said, "Miss Pendergast told me what happened. So I guess I owe you guys. I'll be damned if I can remember a thing after we were about to leave that hotel bar back there."

He spotted the Maxim mounted on the taffrail and added with a crown, "How dare you meddle with the arms shipment in my care! I have to account to El Criado Publico for every single round of ammo!"

Captain Gringo said, "Martha, sit him down somewhere before he falls down on his own." Then, as the redhead steered the skinny American over to a hatch cover, Captain Gringo told him, "We can account for every round pretty good. I just pumped a belt and a half of .30-30 into a Colombian gunboat. You told me it was okay. Don't you remember?"

Bowman sat down, shaking his head to clear it as he

muttered, "No. I don't even remember leaving that damned bar. How in hell could I have given you permission to break out that machine gun? I didn't even know I was aboard until just now! Besides, I would have said no if I'd known what you were asking."

"It's a good thing you were too groggy to know what you were saying, then. The arms and ammo in the hold are slated to fight Colombia, right? Okay. We just fought Colombia pretty good."

Bowman insisted, "You don't understand. I've only been sent along as an observer and noncombatant liaison officer. My orders are not to take part in any fighting myself!"

Gaston said, "Eh bien, should anyone ask, I shall bear witness that you were sleeping the sleep of the just when we saved your unconscious derriere from drowning or worse. Do you really imagine that gunboat crew would have made any distinctions, had they captured you and M'mselle Martha? Mais non, they would have hung you, at least, along with us, from their yardarm. The more attractive demoiselles traveling in our company would no doubt have taken longer to die."

"Don't be ridiculous. Martha and I are American citizens!"

The two soldiers of fortune just exchanged weary glances. There was no point in explaining to an idiot that a Colombian gunboat cruising illegally in Costa Rican waters had orders to play rough.

Esperanza came back on deck carrying a shark billy in one hand and a gunnysack of bran and shredded rope in the other. She looked around, saw that the horizon was visible now, and said, "We located the leak. There is no hope of calking it from inside. But this stuff will swell as it's sucked into the sprung seam."

Captain Gringo shook his head and said, "You can't go over the side."

Martha Pendergast said, "He's right, Señorita Esperanza. I think I saw a shark fin as we came out on deck just now."

Captain Gringo said, "You didn't see *a* shark fin, unless you don't pay much attention to your surroundings."

The redhead followed as Captain Gringo, Esperanza, and Gaston moved over to the rail. A formation of hammerheads was circling the grounded schooner like a Sioux war party. Martha said, "Oh, dear! How many of them are there?"

Captain Gringo said, "One is too many, with hammerheads."

"Heavens, are they man-eaters?"

"They eat women, too. Are you sure you can't plug the leak from inside, Esperanza?"

The big Basque brunette shook her head and said, "I tried. The water pressure simply shoots the calking back in my face. We have to calk that seam before the tide turns, Deek. The almanac promises a spring tide just after sunset. Meanwhile, the sun is shining and they say sharks seldom attack in broad daylight in clear water, no?"

"What do the *sharks* say? Hammerheads may not know they're sharks, anyway. They play to mixed reviews from pearl divers. Nobody knows why their heads are shaped so funny. But they obviously can't have brains shaped the same as other sharks. Why don't we wait until some mako or tiger sharks show up? That way we won't have to guess at their intentions, see?"

Esperanza smiled wanly but said, "That's not funny. I'm going over the side."

"Oh, hell, give me the stuff and I'll do it, doll."

"No, you won't. In the first place, I'm the skipper. In the second, I know more about calking a seam than any handsome landlubber."

They saw that she meant it when she started kicking off har sandals. So Captain Gringo took off everything but his pants, emptied his pants pockets into his hat, and told Gaston to look after everything as he held out a hand and told Esperanza to give him the shark billy.

She said, "Deek, it is foolish to risk two lives when I can make the repairs myself."

He took the billy from her anyway, asking, "Do you have eyes in the back of your head? We'd better use the boarding ladder. The less we splash, the better."

So they did, as everyone else on deck lined the rail, imploring them not to do it. The hammerheads made no comment as they lowered themselves into the clear tepid sea. As Captain Gringo ducked his head under and opened his eyes, they looked bigger, cruising with their sandpaper bellies just above the coral flats all around. Some smaller, darker pilot fish kept the hammerheads company. There were no other fish in sight. Fish were smarter than Esperanza about hammerheads, it would seem.

Esperanza sank until she stood on the bottom with her back to Captain Gringo and the circling sharks and proceeded to shove handfuls of oakum against the bubbling open seam in the *Nombre Nada*'s hull. The bigger target guarding her curves with the pathetic shark billy was running out of air and wondering what to do about it when Esperanza kicked for the surface to inhale some for herself, with the repairs maybe one-quarter done. So he did, too. And when Esperanza went under again he followed.

Their movements near the surface had been unavoidable, since neither had been born with gills. But one of the hammerheads came in to sniff them over, swinging its grotesque head from side to side in curiosity, rage, or whatever in hell went on inside a small flat cold-blooded brain. Captain Gringo got between it and Esperanza and raised the shark billy thoughtfully as he wondered where the hell one poked a hammerhead. The brute's eyes were out on the winglike planes of its weird skull. Its gill slits were protected from frontal attack by the same hammer-shaped head.

The shark apparently hadn't figured him out, either. At the last moment it rolled on its side and veered away, almost scraping the tip of the billy with its long sinister belly. Captain Gringo resisted the impulse to poke it in the guts. He knew *he'd* get mad as hell if someone did that to him.

But up on deck Jim Bowman had risen to join Gaston at the rail. So as he spotted the same shark he drew his pistol from under his jacket. Gaston warned, "Mais non! You could empty that pistol into a shark without even slowing it down. But the splashing and blood in the water could trigger a feeding frenzy!"

Below, Captain Gringo and Esperanza were blissfully unaware of the idiocy above them, but all too aware of the closing circle of sharks, and running out of air again. He followed her up, and as their heads broke water Esperanza gasped, "I think I can finish with one more dive."

He said, "You'd better," and they went under again.

As Esperanza went back to plugging the leak, the same hammerhead or its twin came around the stern, almost trailing a sneaky fin along the hull as it homed in on Esperanza this time. Captain Gringo kicked his own body between the girl and the hammerhead, and when he saw that it didn't seem to want to veer away this time, he stiff-armed the head of the shark billy and let the shark ram its flat head into it. At the same time, a bullet spanged into the water close enough to damn near burst his ear drums!

On deck, Gaston knocked Jim Bowman into the scuppers, drew his own gun, and said softly, "Stay right where you are or I'll kill you! If I see blood in the water I'll kill you anyway, hein?"

Martha Pendergast dropped to her knees by Bowman to shield him as she protested, "You mustn't hurt my Jim, you brute!"

Gaston muttered, "Merde alors," and looked over the side. He saw, to his considerable relief, that the bolder hammerhead had rejoined the Sioux circle to reconsider. Getting poked in the snout and stunned with gunfire had apparently informed its dim mind that whatever those funny things against the hull were, they weren't the usual injured fish one had for supper around here.

Esperanza and Captain Gringo surfaced, the leak plugged at last. To get her up the ladder ahead of him, fast, Captain Gringo goosed her through her wet pants. She gleeped girlishly and told him she'd take him up on that later as she scrambled back aboard. Captain Gringo just made it. One of the hammerheads seemed chagrined to see the party breaking up just as it was getting interesting, and moved in for the kill just a little too late.

As he rolled over the rail, Martha Pendergast said, "You'll have to talk to Gaston, Dick. He hit poor Jim."

Captain Gringo said, "Hello, Gaston. I heard the shot. Felt it, too. My ears are still ringing."

Bowman sat up in the scuppers, protesting, "I was only trying to help."

Captain Gringo said, "Yeah," and took his dry things back from Gaston's free arm as he told the Frenchman, "Put that gun away, for Pete's sake. It's over."

Esperanza took the tall American by a bare wet arm and told Gaston, "I'm leaving you in command here. Deek and me wish for to change out of these wet clothes."

Gaston grinned as he took in how wet indeed Esperanza's clothes were. Her dark nipples and the darker V of her pubic apron were clearly visible through the thin wet cloth. Captain

Gringo said, "Put Bowman back to bed and make sure he stays there this time. He's obviously not thinking clearly yet."

"Merde alors, it would take another four years of college to teach him to tie his shoes. But run along, my children, Papa Gaston has the situation in hand."

They did. Esperanza bolted the door of her stateroom and stripped off everything but her earrings as Captain Gringo dropped his dry things on her built-in desk and let his wet pants just fall wherever they wanted to. Still wet, Esperanza flung herself down on the bedcovers and rolled over to welcome him with open arms and thighs. So he mounted her cool flesh and warmed it up with a good old-fashioned missionary screwing. She liked it that way too. As she hugged him with her big wet thighs she sobbed, "Oh, I was so frightened for us both, and now I am so hot!"

He laughed and said, "So I notice," as he pounded her as hard as he could. The shark scare had raised his own blood pressure, and one of the nicest things about Esperanza was that she was one of the few women a man his size could really let himself go in without having to worry about hurting her. They came together hard, and Esperanza crooned, "Oh, I love the way you make me feel so small and feminine, Deek. I told you the first time we did it how nice it felt to meet a real man, remember?"

He chuckled fondly as he remained in position and said, "Yeah. As I recall, it was sort of an accident. I mistook you for somebody else in the dark when I wandered into the wrong hotel room by sheer accident."

She giggled and said, "It was such a pleasant way to wake up. I knew before I ever saw you with the lights on that you were the answer to a large maiden's prayers. Would you kiss me, por favor? I always feel so romantico when I make love with you, Deek."

He did, gently at first, because he knew what she meant. They'd spoken in the past about what Esperanza called the "magic" between them. Neither of them had ever been dumb enough to call it "love." That was probably why they remained such good friends. But he knew the big tough broad appreciated tenderness. She probably didn't get much from other passing ships in the night. Knockaround guys could be dumb about knockaround dames.

As she kissed back, with growing warmth and probing tongue, he started treating her rough again. There was no sense being *too* tender when a lady dug her nails into one's back and gripped so tightly with her silky wet insides. So they did it again, missionary, and then Esperanza was in the mood for a real orgy. She said, "We've nothing else to do until the tide turns, and we are both so clean and salty. I wish for to try an experiment. A lonely skipper who does not sleep with the crew has time to think up all sorts of naughty tricks, you see."

He said he was game for anything that didn't hurt. So she rolled out from under him and reached in a drawer built into the bulkhead near the head of her bunk bed. She took out an amazingly lifelike but impossibly ample love toy made of black rubber. It looked like someone had cut off the privates of a very well hung Jamaican, balls and all. He laughed and asked, "Is that anyone we know?"

She giggled like a mean little kid and said, "It's my cabin boy. Do you think I could be perverted, Deek?"

"I sure hope so. But your cabin boy makes me sort of jealous. They couldn't have cast that big dong from life."

She rolled on her back, dildo in hand, and assured him, "I

like the real thing much better, Deek. But when one is forced to use a substitute, size helps it make up for lack of romance."

"Okay. Nine out of ten people masturbate and the tenth one's a liar. So how do we manage a ménage à trois with your cabin boy?"

"First let me get him in me, so." She giggled, spreading her thighs wider as she gingerly forced the big, black, amazingly realistic penis into herself. It wasn't easy, even though she was nicely lubricated from his more natural lovemaking, and it looked dirty as hell. He knew he should be ashamed of himself for getting such a hard-on just from watching, but he did, and said, "Hmm, I'm starting to feel left out. What does that feel like?"

She started moving it as she closed her eyes and said, "Heavenly. But not real, yet. Please get on top of me, Deek."

He rolled over to remount her, sort of, but protested, "This is pretty silly, doll. Take that fucking thing out so I can get in."

"In a minute, Deek. I told you one daydreams as one plays with one's self. I have often pretended this was you inside me. I have, I am most ashamed to say, come often with this naughty cabin boy fucking poor lonely me. Now if you would hold me, kiss me, and drive me crazy with this big black penis . . ."

"You're already crazy." He laughed, pressing his bare chest down on her ample breasts and kissing her as he took the base of the dildo from her and proceeded to move it for her. She closed her eyes and moaned, "Oh, it feels like I am making love to two men at once!"

"Yeah? Well, so far *I'm* not getting much of a thrill out of it."

She raised her legs and hooked her ankles around the nape

of his neck, raising her big rump from the damp covers as she sobbed, "Don't stop. You can put it in the other place, if only you don't stop!"

"I thought you said I was too big for you there, Esperanza."

"Did I? I don't care what I might have said when I was *sane*, Deek! At the moment I am inspired to sheer depravity, and, ay ay ay! I am up among the stars and I never wish for to come back down!"

It was driving him nuts, too. So he moved higher up, got his real thing into position, and tried to sodomize her with the idiotic rubber balls of the dildo riding on his pubic bone. She was right about her rear entrance. She obviously hadn't been entertaining her cabin boy or anyone else that way often, if at all. But once he had the head in, he was able to enter fully, and Esperanza started pumping her hips wildly, sobbing, "Oh, my God, I'm being fucked all over!"

She was, too. With the base of the dildo braced against his pubis he was able to move the real and artificial shafts in her as one, and the results were wild as hell for both of them. Her rectum would have been much tighter than her vagina in any case. With that dildo filling every bit of her up front, it felt like he was raping a six-year-old who'd somehow fit into a more than full grown woman's body. He tried to take it easy, but it wasn't easy, and he'd have probably ruined old Esperanza for life had not she sobbed, "Enough! Take it out! Take it all out! I can't stand it feeling so good!"

He whipped the big black dildo out as he withdrew from her rectum, wiped his throbbing prick with the corner of the sheet, and put it where it belonged. She moaned, "Wait! I'm too sensitized! I can't take any more and . . . oh, yes, give me more, more, more!"

So he did, and by the time he came she'd come again, and he came fast, considering it was the third time in a row.

When they'd calmed down enough to talk again, Esperanza pleaded, "Por favor, I don't think I shall be able to walk for a week, and I have to get us off the reef at sunset, Deek."

He wasn't feeling up to entering a track meet, either. So he laughed and rolled off to fumble a smoke and matches from his shirt aboard the nearby captain's desk. He fluffed up the pillows at the head of the bunk bed and lay back to enjoy an after-sex smoke with Esperanza's damp wet head nestled against his shoulder. But after she'd cuddled quietly against him for a time, she sighed and said, "This is so embarrassing. But what you did to my poor little popo has affected me as if I just had a most strong enema, Deek!"

He chuckled and said, "Who goes there, friend or enema?"

She didn't get it. She said, "No fooling, I really have for to take one great shit!"

He sighed and said, "Okay. I'll get up and get dressed, since I assume you have the usual chamber pot under this bunk, right?"

"I do not wish for you to go yet. But I still have to go, myself. Are you sure I won't shock you?"

He laughed and asked, "*How,* for God's sake? I just watched you jerk off in broad daylight, honey bubbles."

She sat up, saying, "That was different. Sex is not the same as heeding the call to nature, is it?"

"What did you think sex was, a call to arms? For God's sake, go ahead and use your chamber pot, doll ass. I won't look, okay?"

She rolled off the bed, reached under it, and pulled out her chamber pot, blushing beet-red as she begged him to close his eyes. So he did. He could smoke just as well with his eyes shut, and he didn't think it could be all that interesting to watch even a lady take a crap.

He couldn't help hearing it, though, as the big Basque

brunette squatted naked on the deck and relieved herself with considerable noise at both ends. She gasped, "Oh, that feels so good. Why is it a thrill to do this in mixed company, do you suppose?"

He said, "Beats me. You're the one doing it. Do you have a damp towel handy, speaking of shit?"

She giggled, told him she thought he was horrid, and washed him off properly as she sat beside him on the bunk bed again. Then she got in between him and the bulkhead to snuggle against him some more as she asked, "Do you know why I enjoy sex so much with you, Deek?"

He said, "Sure. You're concave where I'm convex. How much time do we have left?"

"Not enough. Just hold me, por favor, while I tell you nice things about yourself. You know a woman in my line of work would be a fool to fall in love with any man. So I tell you frankly I have enjoyed many a passing fancy, if not quite as many as you have. But would you think me foolish if I told you that you were the best, so far?"

He patted her bare shoulder and said, "Keep looking. You're still young and beautiful, babe."

She laughed softly and said, "I intend to. If I ever meet a real man hung like my cabin boy I shall probably fall in love with him. Meanwhile, you are the only man I have ever given a shit for."

He laughed, hugged her closer, and removed the claro from his mouth to gently kiss the part of her thick black hair, on her head, before he returned the compliment by saying, "Thank you. I think you're a great lay too. But the thing I like as much about you is that you're a real buddy. I'd just as soon have you at my side in a fight as Gaston, and you're built a hell of a lot better."

"My God, do you screw him in the ass, too?"

"No. But I would, if he was as pretty as you."

The almanac was right about the spring tide. So at sunset, with her screw in reverse, the *Nombre Nada* backed off the reef, apparently undamaged if not improved as the sprung seam clamped tighter on the new calking once the strain was relieved.

Esperanza ordered her Chinese combination ship's surgeon and cook to break out the rations and feed everybody as she set a new course for the hopefully rebel-held Laguna Chiriquí. The trades were picking up again and the sky was once more clear. So as the sun went down with the usual no-crap thud associated with a clear tropic sky, said sky turned star-spangled purple velvet. It would have been more romantic if there had been some dame on board to start working on.

But Esperanza didn't need working on. Her boilers were always full of steam. And Miss Pendergast was spoken for, so what the hell.

He wasn't even thinking about the redhead when he moved forward after supper to drape a tarp over the machine gun mounted in the bows. He was mildly surprised to find her there, alone, staring in wonder over the side at the phosphorescent bow waves of the schooner.

She asked what he was doing and why the sea water seemed to be on green fire. He said, "I don't want this Maxim to rust when and if we take some spray over the bow. The reason said spray glows in the dark like that is bugs. The sea down here is full of funny little microscopic critters that wink on like fireflies back home when air hits 'em. If you really want to see fireworks off the Mosquito Coast, stand by the taffrail of a three-island steamer some night and watch the wake.''

She sighed and said, ''I'm sorry I asked. I thought it was fairy dust in the sea. But it's awfully pretty. Does it do that all night?''

''Yeah, at this time of the year. It can get pretty boring after a while. But at other times of the year it just stays black as ink, so it evens out.''

''Don't you like the tropics, Dick?''

''They're all right, I guess. I'm more comfortable down here than I'd be back in the States right now.''

She sat on the anchor winch, smoothing her skirt primly, and said, ''Jim said they'd hang you back in the States if you ever went back. But I find it hard to believe you're a bad man.''

He said, ''Sometimes I have trouble with that idea myself. While old Jim was blabbing about me, did he mention anything about the pardon I'm supposed to get for doing dumb things for him?''

She nodded gravely and said, ''Yes. The people we're working for are very well connected in Washington. I'm not sure just who they are, but I know one of them's a senator or something.''

He lit another claro to give himself time to consider whatever the hell was going on. He could barely see her, near enough to kiss, and good old Esperanza was at the helm and would stay there until the next watch. But he wasn't as interested in kissing the redhead as he was in what she might or might not know. So he hunkered down near the anchor winch and casually began to pump her for information.

He didn't get much out of her. She was either dumb or

too smart to give away any secrets she might know. She seemed willing to talk. A lot. But she wasn't saying anything he didn't already know. He'd guessed before she told him tht Jim Bowman was in his cabin, feeling lousy. He knew she had her own quarters, near her boyfriend's. He was too polite to ask if this was mere discretion or if old Jim was really stupid enough to marry such a dumb-looking little dame without at least making sure she was good in bed. It could work either way. Now that Captain Gringo didn't have a hard-on, he could tell himself it probably wasn't any of his business.

She asked him how soon they'd make Laguna Chiriquí.

He glanced up at the stars and said, "About this time mañana, weather and gunboats permitting. We should be safe enough until dawn and we're making good time. Come sunrise it gets scary again. We face a full broad-daylight sail with God knows how many Colombian patrol craft anxious to intercept all the goodies in the hold. So pray for more fog by morning."

She said, "Oh, stop it! You're frightening me!"

That had been the general idea. He took a drag on his cigar to let her think it over, if she could, then he said, "Look, sis, you look like a sensible girl. Could I give you some fatherly advice?"

"Pooh, you're not old enough to be my father, Dick."

"Allah be praised. But that's not the point. The point is that I think your best bet would be to stay aboard this tub and go right back to Limón with Esperanza as soon as we unload the cargo. The rebel-held area isn't safe even for a girl like Esperanza, and she's pretty tough."

"I'd say you were right about her, Dick. But Jim says los jurados have that part of Panama securely under control and—"

"Damm it," he cut in, "don't you have anything but bellybutton lint inside your pretty skull, Martha? I know better than to tell you your guy is a dunce, but right now he's nursing a concussion he picked up just trying to *get* to Laguna Chiriquí! Didn't you notice at all when we swapped shots with a Colombian gunboat right outside the harbor? Look, I'll keep it simple. There are trolls under all the bridges ahead, and an army of wolves huffing and puffing at the three little pigs we're delivering this shipment to! I know Jim's your knight in shining armor. But for Pete's sake, the idea is to rescue the maiden *from* the dragon. You're not supposed to deliver her to the damned dragon's lair!"

The little redhead clapped her hands in delight and said, "You're mixing your metaphors. It's so funny, Dick. Do you always tell such amusing bedtime stories?"

He grimaced and said, "Try this one. Once upon a time there was another Panamanian rebel faction called the Balboa Brigade. Gaston and me fought the Colombian army with them. We lost."

"Pooh, you got away, didn't you?"

"It wasn't easy. Most of the brigade didn't. The winners put them up against the wall and shot every one of 'em, after making 'em dig their own graves."

"But not any women, I hope?"

"Men, women, and children, Red. What I'm trying to say is that they play rough as hell down here."

"But Jim and I are American citizens, Dick."

"Honey, you'd be surprised how a bullet goes through a passport. Any passport. Can't you see that if the Colombian military government gave two hoots and a holler about making friends with Americans, this whole damned operation would be pointless? They don't like Yanquis anywhere down here one hell of a lot. The Colombians hate our guts."

He blew some thoughtful smoke out his nose before he added, "In all fairness, I'm not sure they don't have at least a few good reasons. It took the folks down here an awfully long time to get the king of Spain off their backs. I don't remember anybody south of the Texas line inviting Uncle Sam to climb on."

She said, "Pooh, most of the countries down here are run by brutal, bloodthirsty dictators. Isn't it our duty as Americans to bring democracy to one and all?"

"Why should it be? Do the people down here pay taxes to the U.S. treasury or salute the Stars and Stripes? Have they *asked* to be American citizens—second class, of course? I don't see why it's any business of Uncle Sam's whether they want democracy or, hell, Buddhism."

She sniffed primly and said, "I find that a very strange attitude for a notorious soldier of fortune to take! Jim says you and Gaston will fight for anyone who pays you!"

"Sure we will. That's why they call us soldiers of fortune. The point is that we do get *paid*! What I can't understand is a do-gooder who sticks his nose into other people's business just because he thinks God only speaks English. Gaston and me wouldn't have so much work cut out for us down here if only the major powers would butt out. Half the bloodthirsty dictators you're so worried about wouldn't last six weeks if they weren't funded by outsiders."

"Well, my Jim and other true-blue Americans most certainly are not helping those horrid men in Colombia. Don't you *want* to see the Panama Canal dug for your country, Dick?"

He chuckled wryly and said, "That's exactly who wants the canal, Red. Damned few banana growers down where we're going own stock in steamship lines. I'm not against the idea of a canal through Panama. But if I was President Cleveland, I'd cut all this sneaky crap and just go ahead and *do* it!"

"How? The Colombian junta refuses to give permission."

He snorted in disgust and said, "Big deal. They're going to take on the U.S. navy in a gloves-off stand-up fight? You know what I'd do if I was in charge? I'd just go ahead and recognize the Panamanian rebels as a de facto government, send in the gunboats, and tell Colombia to get out of the way so my engineers could dig."

"But that would mean open war and lots of bloodshed, Dick!"

"What do you think gets spilled in all these sneaky funded revolutions, orange juice? The trouble with Uncle Sam is that he wants everybody to like him. But nobody ever likes the boss. You want a guy who's smaller than you to do what you say, you just tell him to do it. You don't hire another mean little kid on the block to beat up his kid sister. If this old tub was a no-kidding U.S. navy gunboat instead of a target, and I had permission to do it right, I could have them digging their damned canal in no time. I'd just put into Panama City, train my turrets ashore, and tell any Colombian authorities who were interested that they had twenty-four hours to choose between a war or the fair price Washington's offered for a canal zone. I doubt if I'd have to fire a shot. If I did, it would all be over long before I can even hope to have those guerrillas we're arming in shape to do anything much. I'd even let you watch the whole power play from the armored bridge. But since somebody State-side wants to do it the hard way, you're going to have to go back with Esperanza."

"That's up for my Jim to say, Captain Gringo."

He nodded, rose, and said, "Yeah. I'd better have a talk with him about it. I can see your pretty skull really *must* be stuffed with bellybutton lint."

It had to wait until morning. He found Jim Bowman fast asleep and Esperanza wide awake when he checked both staterooms. He said, "I thought you were at the helm," as he sat down on the bed beside her and began to take off his boots. Esperanza was of course already undressed. She said, "I don't seem to have my sea legs tonight. So I turned the watch over to Tiavo. He hasn't been ravaged front and back as recently, I'm sure."

Captain Gringo stretched out beside her and took her in his arms and he said, "I feel like someone dragged me through the keyhole backwards, too. Maybe sleep would be a novelty. I can't think of anything else we haven't tried."

She snuggled her lush nude body against his as she murmured, "Are you sure you won't mind, querido? I'm awfully tired, but if you really have to . . ."

He patted her bare rump fondly and said, "Hush, my beautiful Basque bimbo. Right now I couldn't get it up with a block and tackle."

So Esperanza shut up and fell asleep as if he'd punched her in the jaw. He chuckled, lay back, and was wondering if he wanted a last smoke when he passed out with her in his arms.

He slept through the night without dreaming. But then along toward dawn he had a dream to make up for it indeed. It wasn't too clear just how he and the redheaded Martha Pendergast had wound up in the public library together, but there they were, screwing naked as jays in the reading room under a sign that warned: SILENCE! But the redhead kept begging him to pound her harder, and he sure hoped none of those other people using the library this afternoon would notice. So far, nobody seemed to. They all just kept on reading their books at the other tables while he screwed the redhead on this one. She sobbed, "Oh, I'm coming!" and he whispered, "Me too, but can't you read that sign up there?"

Then, when she moaned even louder, he opened his eyes and said, "Oh, hi, Esperanza. I didn't know it was you again."

The passionate Basque girl gripped him tighter with her long arms and legs as she did most of the work, asking him conversationally who on earth he'd expected to meet in her bed. So he didn't think he'd better tell her about his dream. He was almost there himself now, and as he came in her he really couldn't feel disappointed. For if it had felt any better it would have hurt.

As they went limp together he glanced up at the porthole and saw the sky was pearling lighter. He asked her what time it was and she said, "Time to get up, damm it. But thank you for waking me up so pleasantly, querido mio!"

He said, "Don't mention it. One more for the road?"

"Not if you expect me to walk the deck, gracias. I'm still sore from the way you abused me last night, you brute."

He didn't point out that the freak show had been her idea. Women were like that in the cold gray dawn. That was probably why they called it the cold gray dawn. Actually it was sort of warm and sticky this morning.

They washed off, got dressed, and went out on deck. They both grinned as they saw nothing much but fog all around. He walked back to the helm with her and kept her company until breakfast was served to them on trays by the very handy Chinese cook. As they ate alone he asked her if she'd ever tried a Chinaman, and she laughed and said, "Once was enough. It's not true what they say about Chinese men."

He grinned back at her and said it wasn't true what they said about Chinese women, either. He said, "I have to have a chat with Bowman about that dim-witted little redhead."

"Oh? Do you want some of that, Deek?"

"Come on, Esperanza, did I act jealous about your cabin boy, even though he was a little dark for you? I don't want to get under the dumb little dame's skirts. I want her to go back to Limón with you."

Esperanza looked relieved and said, "Bueno. If all else fails, I shall share my cabin boy with her. Laguna Chiriquí is no place for nice girls, or any girls at all, Deek."

He told her he'd just said that and went forward to hunt down the stupid boyfriend of the even stupider redhead. He found them sharing a tray as they sat cross-legged atop the main cabin amidships. Captain Gringo knew Martha had already filled Bowman in when the skinny American said sullenly, "I won't hear of my bride going back to Limón alone! She might not be safe aboard this pirate ship, damm it!"

Captain Gringo stood with his feet on deck, propping his elbows on the cabin coaming as he looked up at them to say, "Esperanza is a gunrunner, not a pirate, and I happen to know she likes boys better than girls. How safe do you figure Martha, here, will be in a guerrilla camp, Bowman? Have you ever spent any time in a guerrilla camp?"

"Of course not. But I've been assured El Criado Publico is a perfect gentleman."

"That well may be. His army is still up for grabs. Revolutions are funny that way. All sorts of people join them, from starry-eyed idealists to habitual criminals who like to call their disgusting habits patriotism."

"I can take care of Martha, damm it."

"I'm sure you can," Captain Gringo lied, adding, "Meanwhile, what about the job you've been sent to do? A liaison officer's supposed to keep track of what's going on. How are you going to manage that if you spend all your time guarding your girl's fair white body from God knows who or what? Oh, I forgot to mention it. Aside from two opposing armies where we're going, the Central American lowland jungle is famous for its reptilian life forms. Only the snakes are poisonous, but the crocs and gators don't need poison fangs to do a job on a well-turned ankle. Have you ever had yellow jack, Martha?"

"Pooh, of course not. Why?"

"Don't worry. You'll learn all about it soon enough if you insist on staying with us. We call it yellow jack because it turns your skin an ugly shade of very sick Chinaman. Its Spanish name is vomito negro. That's because you also get to puke lots of black vomit all over yourself before it kills you, if it kills you. The odds are maybe fifty-fifty, if you're in good shape to begin with. I've already had it. So I can't get it again and, as you see, it didn't kill me. I just *wanted* to die for a while."

The redhead frowned down at him and said, "Pooh, you're just trying to scare me, Dick Walker!"

Captain Gringo said, "That's true. I see I'm not doing so hot. But think it over, kiddies. I gotta go see if we lost our bow gun to green water last night."

They hadn't. Thanks to the tarp, the gun wasn't even starting to rust yet. But he was field stripping it anyway when Gaston joined him, belched, and hunkered down beside him to observe, "Eh bien, if that Chinese cook was only a little less masculine I'd marry him. I have always wanted a Chinese cook, a Japanese wife, and an East Indian mistress."

"What would you do with a wife if you had a great cook and a mistress that liked to get on top, Gaston?"

"True. Forget what I said about the wife. I just passed our bride-to-be and that species of a scarecrow she intends to waste her adorable little self on. Do you suppose that's the only way he can get any of that red hair around his no-doubt ugly rod of amour?"

Captain Gringo agreed and filled Gaston in on his suggestions about the girl going back with Esperanza. Gaston shrugged and said, "Eh bien, you tried. Leave her to heaven, or, for that matter, hell. We have our own adorable asses to look after, and I am beginning to wonder how we're going to manage that. I've been talking with some of the crew, strictly in a platonic fashion, I assure you, and a picture emerges from the mists that I do not fancy."

"Keep talking. I've already figured that Bowman's mysterious backers ain't the real Uncle Sam. I see it as a power play by big-biz guys with maybe the approval of a few congressional war hawks. President Cleveland figures to be sort of surprised if we pull off anything important down where we're going."

"Merde alors, no more surprised than Colombia, I'm sure. Do you recall that adorable Colonel Maldonado who was in charge of the forces we fought the last time we visited Panama, Dick?"

"Yeah, and he's pretty good. That's who we'll be up against again?"

"Oui, and it gets worse. One of the crewmen recalled the real name of this très dramatique Criado Publico. It is Zagal, Professor Fernando Zagal, late of Havana University."

"So? He's a Cuban rebel too?"

"Mais non. He *was* a member of the Cuba Libre movement, but they threw him out. Unfortunately, that's all I know. But there are some très strange people fighting for the Cuba Libre cause, and if they could not use an educated law professor, he must have done something strange indeed, non?"

Captain Gringo snapped shut the Maxim's action and muttered, "Oh boy. Let's hope it was just party politics. Every rebel movement's full of guys who want to be chiefs instead of Indians. At least now I see where they found El Criado Publico. The Cuba Libre movement is being funded and run from New York. He's probably some Cuban exile, somebody from Wall Street found wandering around up there, handing out his own new constitution, and, what the hell, if you can't lead a Cuban revolution lead one in Panama, right?"

Gaston sighed and said, "I wish people who didn't know what they were doing would not do that, Dick. Remember that other fuzzy-minded professor we met up in Mexico that time? The one who meant to overthrow the Diaz dictatorship with a clean mind and lots of speeches?"

"Yeah. I wonder whatever happened to that bunch. They damned near got us killed."

"I know. I was there. Attend me, Dick. If this turns out to be another utopian fantasy, I want your word we shall simply skip out, sans further discussion, hein? I mean it. I am not about to risk my poor old derriere again on people who'd rather make speeches than fight!"

Captain Gringo smiled thinly and said, "Relax. My derriere votes with yours. We'll give it a shot. But if it looks like we're about to get shot for a lost cause, that's it. I've learned the hard way that old Don Quixote was an asshole as well as a nice guy."

"To say a nice guy is an asshole is a redundancy, my child."

It stayed muggy and misty all day. So Esperanza steamed full speed ahead and to hell with light winds and patrolling gunboats. She was right about the new screw being a great improvement. She gave Captain Gringo an even better screw during the siesta hour, although the *Nombre Nada* didn't get to take a siesta. So, as he'd forecast to the redhead the night before, they made it to the rebel-held fishing village at Laguna Chiriquí less than two hours after sundown.

Just how was sort of mysterious. There were neither beacons nor any other indications of the treacherous channel through the mangrove-haunted shallows of the big lagoon. But with Esperanza at the helm they homed in until Captain Gringo, in the bows, spotted a necklace of dim lights ahead at about the same time as the lookout above called down to the big Basque brunette at the helm. Esperanza didn't even have to correct her course as she stopped her engine and coasted in to the now dimly visible pier ahead. A couple of her crewmen ran forward and elbowed Captain Gringo out of their way to cast hawsers to the dimly visible figures waiting for them near a pier stanchion.

By the time the *Nombre Nada* gently bumped the pier fenders they had her too securely fast to bounce back more than a few inches. Captain Gringo nodded with approval and moved aft to see what happened next.

What happened next met with his approval, too. Before he got back to Esperanza in the stern, the guys on shore had a couple of gangplanks of their own in place and some of them were working with Esperanza's crew to break open the hatches.

The big Basque girl was by the rail, making sure the stern lines were secure, when he joined her. He said, "Bueno. Better than I expected, so far. Shall we go ashore?"

Esperanza shook her head and said, "Not until and unless you're invited to, Deek. They have armed guards as well as stevadores on that pier, and they are pretty good, too, but a little trigger-happy. As for me, I am content to remain aboard until we discharge the cargo."

She took his arm and added, in a huskier tone, "It usually takes three or four hours. Shall we go inside for to say adiós properly?"

He laughed and shook his head. He knew he'd hate himself before midnight, because Esperanza was one of those dames a guy never seemed to get enough of, unless he'd gotten enough of her for a while. He said, "I'd love to. But I'd better keep my pants on in case they want me for some reason before you leave."

"Jesus, Maria, y José, I want you for something before I leave! I won't be back for at least a week, querido!"

He was saved from having to plead a headache by Gaston joining them. The little Frenchman said, "A très fatigue juvenile, dressed prettier than a Mexican general, just took Bowman and his redhead ashore. If we don't want Bowman telling tales out of school about us, we had better follow them tout de suite, non?"

Captain Gringo shook his head and replied, "Esperanza her just explained that's not the form. They'll probably send somebody pretty to fetch us, when they want us. Here, have a cigar and hold your horses."

Gaston growled that he had his own smokes and that if he had a horse he'd ride it the hell out of here, adding, "I do not like the ambience here, Dick. Regard how those shadowy stevadores are killing themselves up forward."

"What's the matter with the way they're working the cargo? I think they're doing pretty good."

"They make me très nervous. Nobody works like that in the tropics unless they are full of dope or very very frightened! The officer who came for Bowman and the girl was heavily armed and a typical martinet. We had officers like him in the Legion. They frightened us, too."

Captain Gringo shrugged and asked, "What do you want, egg in your cerveza? We were afraid there wouldn't be enough discipline down here. Now you're bitching because los jurados have good discipline."

Gaston shook his head and insisted, "Mais non, the crew of this trés tight ship has good discipline. But none of them are working hard enough to suffer sunstroke by starlight at the moment! I tell you I hear the dulcet tones of invisible whipcracks, Dick. Those stevadores are run-of-the-mill mestizo peones who, left to their own devices, would work with the slow steady movements of their kind. Ergo, they are either coked to the eyebrows, scared out of their wits, or both!"

The tall American turned to the Basque skipper and asked, "Esperanza?"

She replied, "Don't ask me. I told you I haven't bothered to go ashore. As I said, I give my crew an hour or two shore leave before we leave, depending on the tides. They haven't reported anything particularly frightening along the waterfront."

"How about farther inland?"

"Why should they go farther inland? The cantinas and cathouses are strung along the shoreline."

Gaston said, "That means few outsiders know anything about the settlement itself, then. I know several ports of call on the Barbary Coast that present a smiling mask to the seaside. A tourist can spend a jolly evening along the waterfront at Algiers. But should one venture a block or more into the casbah, and survive, he may leave with a more realistic picture of life among those homicidal lunatics."

He lit his own smoke and pointed the smoldering match shoreward as he added, "The whole place is dimly lit as a North African port of call, too. I don't *like* it here, Dick!"

"Oh, hell, it's a rebel-held area with Colombian gunboats looking to bust all the windows they see brightly lit. You sure have a vivid imagination, Gaston."

"True. That is why I am still alive. At the Siege of Camerone, none of the other Legionaires could imagine the Mexicans winning. As my dear old Tante Ynez, the one who rolled drunks for a living, used to say as she was teaching me about sex and other matters, when in doubt, run like hell!"

Esperanza laughed and said, "I do not think I approve of your aunt's views on child rearing, but she had a point about survival, muchachos. Why don't you just stay aboard and come back to Limõn with me?"

Captain Gringo was too gallant to say that would make the whole trip pointless. But it seemed safe to say a deal was a deal, after he and Gaston had accepted front money. So they chatted awhile as the decking under them vibrated with the heroic efforts of the rebels trying to unload the schooner the day before yesterday, and then it was too late to change their minds.

The same spiffy officer came aboard to get them. He was neatly clad in the Prussian blue uniform of some army Captain Gringo had never met up with before. A crucifix complete with corpus formed the rather odd badge of his peaked cap. But if he was a chaplain he was breaking the rules by wearing that saber and six-gun. He introduced himself strangely; too. He said he was Jurado Numero Ocho and that he'd been sent to escort them up to the Citadel of Justice. So they said adiós to Esperanza and went ashore with him.

There they found an eight-man corporal's squad, with a corporal, waiting for them. As the two soldiers of fortune walked with Jurado Numero Ocho, the uniformed soldados formed a square around them and walked in step with the officer.

Gaston fell into step when he saw Captain Gringo automatically do so, but asked the young officer with the odd insignia if the stoic riflemen were really necessary. Their escort said, "It pays one to be careful, señor. There are always malcontents, and we would not wish for anything to happen to you before El Criado even orders such a thing, eh?"

Captain Gringo made a mental note that the locals called El Criado Publico merely El Criado and didn't ask if that had been a veiled threat. There was no sense giving anyone ideas if it hadn't been.

Jurado Numero Ocho and his men were well legged up, so they didn't even slow down when they hit the steep slope leading up to a vague black mass against the starry sky. The two soldiers of fortune hadn't gotten used to being back on dry land yet, but they were able to keep up without comment, and if this was hazing, stuff it.

They were marched through the gateway of what they now saw to be a big star fort built along seventeenth-century lines. The coral masonry was obviously Spanish, but the layout reminded Captain Gringo of the old French-built Fort Ticonderoga in upstate New York, save for being twice the size of that other colonial frontier outpost. The outer glacis and sloping walls formed a six-pointed star, with gun positions atop the earth-filled triangles. So the interior was a spacious hexagon with lamp-lit quarters, stables, and other buildings facing one another across the central parade. A flagstaff rose from the parade's dead center and, although it was nighttime, a flag fluttered in the trades at the head of the staff. There was just enough light to see the rebel faction's ensign—a gold Latin cross with the scales of justice superimposed on a blood-red field.

The riflemen halted and stayed put as Jurado Numero Ocho led them into a stone-walled building and up a flight of stone steps. He showed them into their adjoining quarters, two rather Spartan cells connected by a common door, and said, "You will wish for to make yourselves presentable before I take you to meet our leader. I shall return for you in fifteen minutes."

Then he turned in place like a puppet with a lollipop stick up its ass and left them to their own devices.

Lamps were already burning in both rooms. So they could see they'd been provided with comfortable-looking four-posters, complete with mosquito netting—vital for these parts. A full-dress Prussian blue officer's kit was neatly folded on each bed. In addition, they'd both been issued one chest of drawers, one washstand with mirror nailed to the stucco wall above, one bentwood chair, and one large, very realistic crucifix on the same spot on the wall of each room. The two rooms were in fact mirror images of each other.

Gaston closed the door to the corridor, shrugged, and said, "Eh bien. He said fifteen minutes. I hope they have my size right."

He ducked into his own quarters to find out as Captain Gringo began to undress. He'd shaved that morning aboard the *Nombre Nada*, but when he saw they'd issued him a new toilet set as well as a full basin of water and an olla holding more of the same, he picked up the lamp and went over to check out his jaw in the mirror.

Captain Gringo still had sea legs, and the planks of the floor were uneven. So he snagged a heel on a warped plank and spread his arms wide to recover his balance. He had no trouble with that part, but he managed to snuff the lamp by waving it around like that.

He could still see well enough to put the lamp on the chest of drawers, thanks to the light from Gaston's open door. But now it was too dark in here to shave or even to see if he needed a shave. So he reached into his pants pocket for a match.

But before he relit the lamp, a pinpoint of light where no pinpoint of light should have been caught his eye. He frowned and moved closer to see why light was shining through a stone wall at least six inches thick.

The wall had been cracked and replastered more than once, thanks either to the frequent earthquakes or to the occasional pirates of the recent past. As he examined the mysterious dot of light more closely, he saw that while the plaster on his side was almost whole, a chink had fallen or been dug out from the other side. He put his eye to the pinhole. He saw another four-poster, covered with red satin and surrounded by an expanse of plush oriental carpet. The bed was unoccupied. He couldn't see enough to tell if the whole room was. He learned it wasn't when the naked torso of a well-built woman moved across his line of sight.

He caught only a quick glimpse of her from pubic V to proud firm breasts before she moved out of sight again. He took it on faith that there had to be some other parts attached and that her face and legs had to be at least okay to go with what he'd seen. He also doubted very much, now, that the hole in the wall had been planned as an espionage device.

Had the lady next door noticed it before he had, she'd hardly have been parading around her boudoir bare-assed.

He grinned and helped himself to some soap from the washstand to plug the pinhole on his side, lest she trim her own lamp and notice it before he could at least see her face as well, at a more convenient time.

Then he relit his own lamp, decided his stubble wasn't bad, and got out of his rumpled linen pants and into the blue uniform they'd provided. It fit perfectly. There was no telegraph line down the Mosquito Coast. So they'd either been very good guessers or they'd known in advance that he and Gaston were going to be contacted in San José.

He knew it had been the latter when the little Frenchman came in to rejoin him, looking dapper as hell in a perfectly fitting smaller outfit.

Gaston said, "I see they have yet to issue us sidearms. But I have my adorable .38 under this tunic anyway. Does it show?"

"Not enough to matter. Does mine?"

"Mais non. But anyone who knows you well enough to choose your clothes would hardly expect you to meet total strangers unarmed. What do you make of the religious overtones to this operation, Dick? I am of course a Catholic, when I think about such matters at all. But I confess it never occurred to us in the Legion to nail crosses to our barracks wall."

Captain Gringo shrugged and said, "Hispanics take such things more seriously than you frogs. It doesn't bother me. I wouldn't want this to get around, but we heretics have crosses on at least some of our church steeples back home."

They were saved further religious discussion by Jurado Numero Ocho coming to get them. He led them past the mysterious naked lady's bedroom door, then past a lot more doors until they entered a cavernous room that seemed to be trying to make up its mind whether it was an office or a grotto.

A single oil lamp burned on a huge oak desk, its rays barely making it to the rough stone walls all around. But they could see the silver-haired, black-clad man rising from behind it to circle around and greet them. El Criado Publico, it couldn't have been anyone else, was a tall, distinguished-looking man of about sixty, dressed, unlike his followers, in the civilian clothing of a Spanish hidalgo. He walked as only a drunken American banker or a Spanish hidalgo walked, giving off waves of grave dignity as he waved his hand at the two comfortable-looking leather chairs facing his desk and said, with a warmer smile than one might have expected, "Please be seated, caballeros."

As they did so, their host turned to the officer who'd brought them and softly suggested that his guests might require refreshments. Jurado Numero Ocho saluted, whirled around, and took off like a scalded cat.

El Criado chuckled softly and moved sedately back around the big desk to take his own seat before he said, with a faint smile, "I have already spoken to our friend from los Estados Unidos, Señor Bowman. Ah, he has informed me the shipment will not tally with the bill of lading this time, due to your, ah, unauthorized use of some of it."

Gaston snorted in disgust and answered, "Merde alors, your precious cargo would be on the bottom of the sea at this moment, along with Bowman as well as ourselves, had not Dick here hosed a Colombian gunboat down with a small part of it!"

El Criado Publico nodded gravely and turned to Captain Gringo with an expectant smile. The tall American said, "I thought we had that settled. I see Bowman's one of those guys who covers his own ass first. I asked his permission to break out two Maxims and some ammo. I guess he forgot. He was semiconscious at the time."

"Es verdad? Señor Bowman did not mention giving you permission, Captain Gringo. He tells me he told you not to trifle with the shipment at all."

Captain Gringo took out a cigar and held it up unlit to ask, "Permiso?" and, when the older man nodded silently, lit up before he leaned back and said, "Let's save time and call me a liar. The point is that you guys hired me to fight Colombia for you. I put at least six or eight Colombian seamen out of action for sure, and maybe saved la *Nombre Nada* and the rest of the shipment for you. So sue me."

El Criado Publico chuckled and replied, "That could be dangerous, if half of what I have heard of you is true, Captain Gringo. I just wished for to clear the matter up. I am satisfied you did the right thing. Just between the three of us, I have the impression your Señor Bowman is muy estupido at best and may present us with some problems. But I am required for to be nice to him, lest my backers in New York suspect I am the difficult person my enemies say I am."

He waited expectantly, saw that neither had any comment to offer, and added, "You both know, of course, that some former comrades of mine in the Cuba Libre movement have been telling wicked lies about me?"

Gaston shrugged and replied, "Oui, I heard something to the effect that they had different views than yourself. The exact details escape me. I confess I have not been following current events in Cuba."

El Criado Publico shook his head wearily and said, "They are all quite mad, you know. They accuse me of being, ah, eccentric. But I tell you they will never establish anything but another pathetic little banana republic up in Cuba unless they mend their ways."

They forgot to ask him what the Cuba Libre guys were doing wrong when the door opened and a Negro came in with a silver tray of wineglasses and a carafe of red Madeira. The servant placed the tray on the desk and crawfished out. So El Criado Publico poured as he said, "Cuba is ancient history. My dream of an ideal republic will work just as well here in Panama. But, as I said, we must treat this Bowman with tact no matter how we may feel about him, eh? It's no great secret my Yanqui backers are not interested in my dreams because they admire my no-doubt amusing Spanish accent. I make no secret of the fact I am using them as well. But I am dealing, as they say, from the top of the deck. I intend to let them dig a canal, or a hole to China, for all I care, once my Republica de Panama is set up according to my own advanced theories. To do that I must have money and other weapons of modern warfare. So be nice to Señor Bowman, por favor. As I said, I have enemies who do *not* deal from the top of the deck, and it is most important he gives us a favorable report, eh?"

Captain Gringo said, "You're the boss. While he was ratting on us, did Bowman mention what I said about him bringing that dumb redhead along?"

The older man chuckled and said, "He did. I confess in my younger days I might have brought Señorita Pendergast along myself. But I am too old and far too dedicated to my dreams to concern myself with such matters now. I agree the man is a fool. But the girl should be safe enough. We have female dependents with us and I assure you none of my followers would dare to trifle with her. As a matter of fact, I have my own daughter, Inocencia, here with me. I was afraid to leave her alone in New York at the mercy of my former friends."

Captain Gringo didn't comment. He knew all to well that Latins tended to drag women along on military expeditions, and they got so unhappy when you told them they were stupid.

Gaston asked about the guns that might go with the shells just delivered, and El Criado Publico said, "I have been promised a battery of field guns. That's another reason we must be nice to Señor Bowman."

"Merde alors! Don't we have any artillery at all?"

"Not at the moment, alas. But so far, through the grace of God, no Colombian land forces seem to be headed our way, and meanwhile we have plenty of small arms, the machine guns you two came down with, and all the ammunition we could possibly need, no?"

Captain Gringo said flatly, "No. There's never enough ammo when you need it. Whose idea was it to hire us, sir? I got the impression it couldn't have been Bowman."

The older man laughed and said, "He and the other Yanquis were dead set against it, as a matter of fact. But I insisted. I know you both by repute more than you apparently know me, eh?"

That was true. So Captain Gringo didn't answer. Gaston asked, "May one ask about the species of presidential pardon they promised my young friend here?"

El Criado Publico said, 'I insisted on that, too. One can hardly establish a reputable republic with the help of a wanted criminal, eh?"

Gaston said, "Oui, that would seem perhaps a bit gauche in the history books. But we were told the pardon would be conditional on the success of this interesting project."

The would-be father of his country nodded sadly and explained, "I said not everyone is dealing as fairly as myself.

But at any rate I did get them to agree to a pardon, once you've helped us rid our land of Colombian tyranny."

Captain Gringo asked, "What if they double-cross us? Don't bother about what happens if we lose."

El Criado Publico said firmly, "They will have to give you the pardon they promised, if they want me to give them the rights to their canal. On that you can depend. You have my word."

"I'm sure it's good, sir. But I don't know about theirs! Does old President Cleveland even *know* about this deal down here?"

The older man's face went blank as he answered softly, "Let us simply say certain senior members of his party do. Never fear. If they betray our trust, I can always issue you a pardon myself, and we can dig the canal ourselves and keep all the tolls, no?"

Before Captain Gringo had to think up an answer, the door opened once more and both soldiers of fortune managed, just, not to gasp aloud at the sight of what was coming in.

A regal young woman with chestnut hair, that odd ripe peach complexion only certain high-born Spanish women ever seemed to have,and a figure Captain Gringo remembered last from seeing it through a pinhole, was standing in the doorway, dressed now in black velvet. But that was only part of the surprise. She was leading a full-grown black jaguar on a leash. The big cat matched her dress perfectly, but the way it was staring at them with those big yellow eyes made them wonder how good a grip she had on that damned skinny leash!

The girl said, "Father, you are preventing us from dining and I am most hungry. The other guests are waiting too."

El Criado Publico rose with a sheepish smile and introduced her to them as his daughter, Inocencia Zagal. That wasn't half as surprising as her choice of pets. She returned their greeting with a polite cold smile and eyes about as friendly as her black jaguar's. But neither of them bit anybody as they all went out and down the corridor to the dining room.

There they found Bowman and Martha Pendergast already at table, with a half-dozen officers dressed like Numero Ocho. When the one nearest the head of the table was introduced as Numero Uno, it was easy to see why Numero Ocho had to be left out. There just weren't enough chairs for that many Numero Guys.

El Criado Publico took his place at the head of the table. His daughter sat at his right. Where in hell that big cat might be under the table at the moment was something to think about. But as servants began serving the first courses, none of the other guests seemed to be having their shins gnawed, so Captain Gringo decided just to enjoy the meal.

Neither he nor Gaston made a habit of discussing blood and slaughter at the dinner table, but the redhead across from him kept asking dumb questions about the current situation. Their host looked pained and said, "I am not the military expert here, señorita. I am more intent on my new constitution at the moment. But perhaps one of my younger associates could inform you about our present battle lines, eh?"

He shot a look at Numero whatever seated between Captain Gringo and Gaston, and the officer, juror, or whatever the hell he thought he was, smiled across the table at Martha and said, "At the moment we control an area of several hundred square kilometers, señorita. We have pushed our lines over ten kilometers into the jungles to the southeast without encountering any enemy resistance."

Gaston muttered, "At least we might be out of artillery range," and Captain Gringo kicked him under the table to shut him up. He kept his own mouth shut to listen with some interest as the man who knew a lot more than he did continued, "We of course have scouting patrols even farther out. Apparently the Colombian armed forces are afraid to attack us."

Captain Gringo went back to concentrating on his meal, which made a lot more sense. Gaston opened his mouth to say something about their old pal Colonel Maldonado, but decided not to. He and Captain Gringo didn't need to be told that Maldonado was a tough pro who would attack in his own good time and didn't scare easy. Probably nobody else at the table wanted to hear that.

Bowman said something about the local natives under rebel control, and El Criado Publico assured him, "You may tell your friends up north that we have the full support of the local populace. I have already instituted certain reforms and the results have been most encouraging. All these local peones needed was a firm hand on the reins and even justice, for a change."

Someone in the back of Captain Gringo's brain said, "Oh boy!" and he couldn't help asking just what the erstwhile law professor meant by a firm hand on the reins.

The silver-haired man at the head of the table smiled in a fatherly way as he explained, "You know how unfairly this isthmus has been governed up to now by the junta in the distant Andes to the south. When they are not seizing the poor Panamanians' few centavos for so-called back taxes, they neglect them entirely."

"That's bad? No offense, but most of the poor people I meet down here tell me they just wish everyone would leave them alone."

El Criado Publico sighed and said, "Of that I have no doubt. In a world of angels, neither laws nor government of any kind would be needed. Alas, we do not live in a world of angels, and unwashed half-breed illiterates need to be governed indeed. When we first took over here, we found the local natives living little better than savages in a dog-eat-dog society of blood-feud, banditry, and, forgive me, señoritas, sexual depravity."

What the two soldiers of fortune were thinking must have shown, because their host quickly added, "Do not take me for a prude, por favor. I know boys will be boys, as you Yanquis say, and while my own morality may seem old-fashioned to some, I know better than to impose it on others. But surely any reasonably person mist admit there must be *some* limits."

His daughter, Inocencia, said demurely, "What my father is trying to say is that some of the niggers were living in sin with their sisters, daughters, or little boys. One village bully made a practice of raping six-year-old girls. He doesn't do that anymore."

Her father protested, "Inocencia, you are speaking in mixed company!"

She shrugged and stuffed her mouth with a roll. Across the table, Bowman was looking uncomfortable. But his redheaded intended just looked interested as she asked brightly, "How do you feel about *consenting adults* just, well, living in sin, sir?"

The old man pursed his lips and said primly, "That is a matter one must, alas, leave for them and their God to decide, provided of course we are speaking of normal relationships between members of the opposite sex."

"The Church used to burn queers at the stake," said Inocencia, adding, "Tell them what *you* do to them, father."

Her father said firmly, "That is enough, by the Virgin's blush! It is time to change the subject, señores y señoritas.

This is after all a Christian household and we are at the table!''

So the redhead, to change the subject to something less controversial, said, ''I notice lots of crosses around here. Are you people all Roman Catholics? I'm a Methodist myself.''

Captain Gringo would have kicked off her knee cap under the table if he'd been able to reach it. But it didn't seem to bother their host, who looked relieved, in fact, as he smiled down the table at Martha and told her, ''Naturally most of my followers are of the faith. But I assure you our symbol merely means we stand for the Christian values all good Christians and, indeed, good Jews and Moslems should accept. My proposed constitution for all Panama grants complete religious freedom to all. Within reason, of course. I doubt if even your great American Constitution allows human sacrifice or other criminal acts in the name of religious freedom, eh?''

The redhead smiled and said, ''Oh, that sounds fair. Don't you think it sounds fair, Jim?''

Her escort, to his dubious credit, murmured, ''Martha, will you just shut up?''

''Pooh,'' she pouted, ''What did I say?''

Another course was served. Then another, and another. Hispanics who could afford it liked to dine late and just keep dining until the food ran out or somebody burst. As the meal wore on, and on, even Martha was getting too heavy in her seat to chatter. Like many Americans, she didn't know the kitchen help would get the leftovers for their own late meal and so she ate every platter clean like the good little girl she thought she was being. Captain Gringo left half of his on the plates and still felt like he needed a new belt before dessert, thank God, was finally served.

He braced himself for the usual retirement to the drawing

room for brandy and cigars. But their host said, "I know you must all be most tired from your long sea journey, while I, forgive me, have work on my desk that will keep me there past midnight. So would I be rude if I suggested we call it an evening?"

Nobody saw [illegible] argue with that. As that started getting to their feet, Numero something or other told Captain Gringo he'd show him around in the morning and offered to escort him back to his quarters. The taller American said he could manage and got out of there before the redhead could say something uncomfortable or the chestnut-haired Inocencia could drag that big cat out from under the table by its tail.

Gaston agreed it felt like they'd been stuffed as the two of them made it back to their quarters, split up, and hit the sack.

It had been a long day. So Captain Gringo fell asleep within minutes. But it had been a long dinner and it wasn't sitting well. So he woke up, he didn't know when, and sat up to belch. He started to lie back down. Then he heard the same funny sound he'd thought he'd been dreaming, whatever the hell it was.

It sounded like an animal growling. A *big* animal growling, deep in its throat, and someone was whispering to it.

He belched again and got up in the dark, nude, to move over to the wall and pop the soap plug out of the pinhole for a look-see.

What he saw convinced him he was still asleep and dreaming.

On the bed next door, the well-stacked Inocencia had taken her clothes off again and was naked on her back atop the red satin bedcovers. The big black jaguar was on top of her, screwing her like a man as it pawed her naked breaths with sheathed paws and growled, or purred awfully loud, in time with the lashes of its tail and thrusting black velvet rump.

The girl's eyes were closed and she wore a dreamy *Mona Lisa* smile as she ran her nails up and down the big cat's spine, whispering, "Ay, mas, mas Diablo mio!"

It was enough to give a man as well as a jaguar an erection, but old Diablo had seen her first and Captain Gringo didn't think he'd want to go sloppy seconds to a cat in any case. So he just watched, trying not to laugh, as the innocently named Inocencia acted in a way he found it hard to believe her father would have approved of.

She must have found it less disgusting than Captain Gringo did, because the next thing he knew she'd wrapped her long shapely legs around her feline lover and was kissing the big cat on its open mouth, running her tongue over the jaguar's big ivory fangs as it panted in passion. He muttered to himself, "She's either got that damned thing trained pretty good, or she's nutty as a fruitcake!"

It was hard to resist the impulse to rush next door, not to screw her but to rescue her. A lady animal trainer had told him once that even smaller wild cats made unreliable pets. Though, come to think of it, she hadn't been screwing that tiger who'd left those scars on her thigh, to hear her tell it. Maybe sex had a calming effect on big cats. It was starting to have a calming effect on him, watching. For though the perverse Inocencia was pretty as a picture and built like a Greek goddess, there was something repellent going on in there under those chestnut ringlets. It was more than the beastiality. Anyone could get hard up, and her father was obviously too strict for her to get many shots at the real thing. But she wasn't using her dangerous pet as a *substitute* for normal sex. As she kissed the brute's mouth and crooned endearments to it as she thrust her body in response, he sensed she was actually accepting Diablo as her lover!

He grimaced and plugged the hole again to light a smoke. He was wide awake now, and, as he'd warned himself earlier, he was hurting for old Esperanza again. He sat on the edge of the bed with a wry chuckle, wondering what Esperanza would say to a roll in the hay with a real beast. He'd known a blonde one time who'd let her police dog have some once in a while, as a practical way to keep it from annoying guests, she'd said. He hadn't liked the idea much. A hotel dick back home had also assured him it was a known fact that any lady checking in alone with a large male dog was surely a loving mistress indeed. The dick hadn't said how he knew. Probably there were lots of peepholes nobody knew about. Hotel dicks led disgusting lives.

He got up, muttering to himslf, "Come on, you idiot, what do you expect to see? Once you've seen a lady screw a jaguar, you've seen a lady screw a jaguar, right?"

He held his lit cigar down at his side and unplugged the pinhole for another peek. He almost dropped the cigar on his bare feet when he saw what Inocencia was doing now.

She had the big cat on its back, purring, as she crouched over it, fingering herself between those wasted creamy thighs as she gave it oral sex. The sight of those lush human lips sliding up and down the vividly pink beastial shaft definitely cooled off any desire he might have had ever to kiss Inocencia, even in a brotherly fashion.

He plugged the hole again, vomited in the washbasin, and went back to bed resolved never to peek in on her again. He knew, of course, that he would. But now he was certain that whatever El Criado Publico might be, his daughter was nuts for sure.

He began to feel better about the nutty Inocencia's father after he'd had breakfast. Breakfast had been a bitch, with

Inocencia sitting across from him looking like butter wouldn't melt in her mouth. He just didn't want to think about what cat come might taste like.

The Numero who took them out to show them around was Numero Cuatro. It was hard to keep track. They all looked like El Criado Publico had recruited them from the same military school. He probably had. His young officers were all eager and devoted to him and his theories, whatever they were. Captain Gringo was a little cynical about utopias. The poor slob who'd made up the name had wound up getting his head chopped off.

The spiffy uniforms were reserved for the officers and personal guard of the Presidente-to-be. When they went to inspect the regular rebels, they found them dressed like any other guerrillas, or bandits, south of the Texas line. At least their Krag rifles were new, and someone had shown them how to keep them clean and carry them without dropping them in the dust. Numero Cuatro said they'd had some practice on the range but that everyone was depending on him and the machine guns when and if.

Captain Gringo told the young zealot, "Back up and run that past me again. In the first place, I can only fire one, okay; two machine guns at a time. In the second place, I was told we were coming down here to *teach* people, not to fight 'em!"

Numero Cuatro nodded brightly and said, "Sí, you will teach us how to make war until we have to make war, and then you will show us how to kill the enemy, no?"

"No, I hope. But let's get the show on the road, at least."

He turned to Gaston and said, "Pending the arrival of at least one fucking field gun, how do you feel about acting as drill officer while I instruct at least some damned body on automatic weapons? We have a dozen machine guns, Allah be praised. If we can set up a dozen machine-gun squads that know which way to aim, we'll be that much ahead."

Gaston shrugged and replied, "I see they already know how to dress to the right and cover down. I take it we are talking about teaching them more advanced infantry tactics?"

"Right. Try to pick some likely noncoms as you bully them, this time. There's no way the two of us are gonna lead 'em all, even if we get dumb."

He turned to Numero Cuatro and asked how many troops they had, all told. The pretty young officer said, "About eight hundred. Forgive me, I know you are experienced in such matters, but we already have our officers and noncoms picked."

"No shit? Okay. What's the first order an assistant squad leader gives when a shell whizzes in and blows the squad leader and a couple of other riflemen to hash?"

"I beg your pardon, Captain Gringo?"

"That's what I thought. For the record, when in doubt, always advance on the guns shelling you. Why do we always try to take the high ground?"

"Uh, *do* we, Captain Gringo?"

"Great. Are you listening, Gaston?"

"Oui, sans astonishment. They spend more time on military courtesy at most military schools. Eh bien, leave the basic infantry tactics to me. Aside from being the greatest artillery man in the world, I am one of the few Legion infantrymen who made it out of Camerone alive."

So they got to work.

It wasn't easy. But within a few days they began to see some improvement in the rebel army as Gaston whipped the privates into fighting shape without having to fight too many of them, and Captain Gringo instructed the officers and noncoms in the finer points of machine gunning. There was more to it than learning how to load a Maxim and hose it at the countryside in general without it exploding in your face from an improper headspacing. The weapon was new, and many people still thought you just had to aim it like a firehose and everybody on the other side just fell down.

The Maxims had to be set up right. They fired six hundred rounds a minute. That meant that if one traversed too fast, the bullets swept the front spaced up to six feet apart, and a lot of charging infantry could pour at you through a six-foot gap. It made more sense to aim stationary streams from two guns in a shallow X between one's position and the enemy advance. Hardly anybody was going to wade through *that*.

He pointed out that a machine gunner was only a machine gunner, not God, and that the other guys might have guns too. One rifle bullet was all it took to put out the lights of an overconfident automatic-weapons man. So, aside from setting up to blow the other side away, a well-placed machine-gun nest had to be a tough target and hard to get at. He taught them the advantages of at least half a squad of riflemen assigned to each machine-gun nest to pick off wild men charging in from outside its field of fire. He insisted that such backup consist of picked sharpshooters, not cast-off fuck-ups volunteered by their old squad leaders.

The choir-boy young officers and older tougher-looking noncoms were willing pupils, wherever los jurados had gotten them. Gaston reported that his riflemen caught on fast, too, and that none of them seemed to be local natives. At least a dozen of them had taken part in a losing fight with Diaz in the south of Mexico. A couple had fought in

Nicaragua for the losing Granada side. Most seemed to be Cubans, and they said they were tired of losing, too. Gaston said they wouldn't, again, if only they'd learn to keep their heads up and their asses down.

The nights were less fun.

Sometimes there was no light at all in Inocencia's bedroom. Sometimes when Captain Gringo unplugged the peephole her bed was empty or she was simply reading a book or buffing her nails. Not even a sex maniac spent all their time on sex. But when she got the urge, Inocencia made up for lost time in ways that made the American watching wonder if maybe he wasn't a sex maniac too, for watching. The chestnut-haired Spanish beauty had a hell of an imagination. Her jaguar lover was probably just a horny oversized tom cat who did as he was told. They sure could get in the damnedest positions. He quit for a while when she wound up with her wide-open groin facing his pinhole, unoccupied, as she sucked off her feline lover with its fuzzy black balls and winking pink asshole facing him too. He'd figured out by now why they never went sixty-nine. Even little house cats had sandpaper tongues. As it was, the chestnut-thatched open vagina also winking at him looked a little raw from overwork.

El Criado Publico had given him a book, privately published in New York, outlining his utopian views on the ideal state. So he plugged the hole, lit his lamp, and decided to read himself to sleep in bed instead of jerking off. There were no female servants up here in the fort, and he didn't know where the redheaded Martha Pendergast was bedded down, alone or with her intended. She'd asked El Criado Publico if he was a justice of the peace, and he'd told her, nicely, not to be ridiculous.

Captain Gringo understood this better as he read the old man's book on what he called "equal justice for all." As an ex-lawyer of the old Spanish school, Zagal didn't hold with bending the rules a fraction of an inch for anybody. He held that once you made allowances for one special circumstance, you might as well throw the whole legal code aside and rule by royal whim. The ancient Romans had been right about justice being a blind goddess who simply weighed the evidence on her scales of justice and either swung her sword or didn't.

Captain Gringo started humming "Give Me That Old Time Religion" as he turned the pages rapidly, skimming the rather repetitious text, until he came to where El Criado Publico had written:

"It is a wicked myth to accuse the Grand Inquisitor, Torquemada, of needless cruelty. His fellow Dominicans record that Torquemada often wept after ordering criminal heretics to the stake, and it is known he considered gentler forms of execution. But the laws of Torquemada's time specified Death by Fire for relapsed heretics, and the Grand Inquisitor was above all a man of dedication to the *Law*. His enemies forget that he in fact pardoned far more people than he ever burned, and ordered pregnant women strangeled before the flames reached them. The end result of the Grand Inquisitor's evenhanded policy was, as we know, a country again peacefully united under one faith. Consider, if you will, the years of religious strife in France, Germany, and other lands rent by the dire results of allowing any misguided malcontent to spawn his or her own religion, and you will see how, in the end, the handful of heretics executed in Spain saved a million lives or more. Thanks to Torquemada, the Iberian Peninsula never suffered anything like the Thirty Years War, in which at least a third of the population of Germany perished!"

Captain Gringo shrugged and read on. That wasn't the way

the Spanish Inquisition was described in Connecticut schoolbooks. But, in fairness, American schoolbooks were mostly written by New England Protestants.

He found it harder to buy, "Justice must not only be sure. It must be dealt out in a manner that the common man, who is all too often an impulsive child, can understand. Punishment must fit the crime, not as punishment as much as *example*. Once you allow the illiterate mind to even hope for acquittal on appeal on some technicality beyond his or her grasp, all respect for the law vanishes. A killer must be killed no matter who is killed or why. Other criminals must be punished swiftly and severely, with no discussion of extenuating circumstances. That is all the uneducated mind understands. The English myth, Robin Hood, is one of the most subversive books ever written and has no doubt been the inspiration for countless savage criminals like the late Americano bandit Jesse James. The poor shall always be with us and the poor shall always need money. They must be constantly warned that it is simply wrong to steal and that they shall be punished if they do so!"

Captain Gringo skipped a few chapters to see if the old guy had anything to say about running his utopia for anyone who escaped the gallows. Zagal had said he was working on a constitution for Panama. That was probably why it wasn't in this vanity publication. He got tired of reading about how dumb everybody else was. So he put the book aside to catch some sleep. Between the views of El Criado Publico and his daughter, next door, his dreams that night were pissers.

In the morning Gaston woke him up with some half-assed plan about the up-to-now-useless four-pound shells they had on hand. The morning sky was greenish and the air smelled like brass polish, so Gaston was probably right that Esperanza wouldn't make another run before the hurricane somewhere off shore either hit or went somewhere else.

They went down the hill to the village. Gaston was looking for a machine shop. They didn't find one when they asked around, although everyone was anxious as hell to help them find one. They had drinks at a cantina, and when they tried to pay, the waiter refused their dinero.

He said there was indeed a blacksmith down the quay who sometimes did heavy work for the local boat builders. When they left, Captain Gringo left a tip on the table. The waiter caught up with them and begged them to take it back, explaining, "Gratuities are forbidden under the new law of Panama, señores."

The tall American took his money back with a puzzled smile and they continued on. Gaston said, "Très unusual, non? These blue uniforms seem to open every door around here. I wonder where the nearest whorehouse is."

"I thought you were looking for someone to build you a cannon."

"Oui, but even dirty old men need more than their own fist to calm their nerves. If all services here are gratis to the armed forces, one could *call* it romance, non?"

They reached the blacksmith shop first. The smith was almost as tall as Captain Gringo and built like a gorilla. He looked mean enough to whip them both fair and square, but he acted meek as a lamb facing a pair of timber wolves as they showed him Gaston's rough sketch of what they wanted and asked the smith if he could make it.

The burly smith spread the drawing on his anvil and studied it as if it were his own death sentence before he licked his lips and said weakly, "Forgive me, señores, I have a wife and children."

Gaston said, "Eh bien, congratulations. Do you think you can forge this crude weapon for me as well?"

The smith fell to his knees on the cinders at their feet and sobbed, "I would if I could, I swear to God, señores! But I have never attempted to hammer that much iron together, and even if I could improvise the barrel, I do not have the machine tools it would require to form your ever so wondrous breech block."

Captain Gringo held out a hand and said, "For God's sake, get up and stop whimpering, hombre. You don't have to be afraid of us. We don't bite."

The smith looked unconvinced as he allowed Captain Gringo to help him back to his feet. The American was aware of the man's sheer strength as their hands gripped. But he was sure that if he asked the poor guy to drop his pants, bend over, and spread his cheeks, he'd get no argument. Gaston said, "Eh bien. Forget the breech and let us discuss the tube. Could you not hammer strap stock around a hardwood mandrel the diameter of the shells and then simply burn the wood out with your forge? The charred-out wood would carbonize the inner layers of wrought iron to mild steel as well, non?"

The smith began to look interested, despite his obvious fear of them. He said, "Sí, but what about the rifle lands, señor?"

Gaston shrugged and answered, "Smooth bore will have to do, sans a respectable machine shop in this très fatigue little village. How far can one fire into a jungle in any case, hein? Wait, let me rephrase the breech block with my ingenious pencil stub. Do you think you could at least manage something like the barrel bolt for a door, on a larger scale of course?"

The smith said he was sure willing to try. Captain Gringo looked at Gaston's new design and said, "This looks pretty risky, Gaston. Without threads, you'd be taking all the recoil on one skinny bar of mild steel."

"True. But that is how they fashioned the first breech loaders, back in the 1600s, non?"

"Yeah, and then they went back to muzzle loading for a couple of hundred years. They must have gotten tired of having big guns blowing up in their faces. Leave us not forget that those old treacherous breech loaders fired black powder, too! Those four-pounder rounds use cordite, maybe six or eight times as powerful!"

Gaston said to let him and the smith worry about it. Said smith had dropped everything and was already heating up strap stock as they left. He'd said the mandrel was no problem. There was a shipwright down the quay who'd be glad to lathe-turn the wood for them, at no cost and poco tiempo. He had a wife and children too.

As they moved up the walk, Captain Gringo asked, "Do you get the impression folks are scared of us in this neck of the woods, Gaston?"

The Frenchman nodded and replied, "Us or these uniforms. I told you when we arrived that those dock workers moved like someone was holding a gun to their heads."

Captain Gringo took out a smoke and lit up before he said, "I think you might have had a point. It's funny, I don't see anyone else in these pretty duds policing the village.But the villagers act like there's a drunken rurale on every corner. A mean one. Old Zagal and his kid jurados don't *act* very tough though."

"Neither did the Borgias, when people behaved as they'd been told, Dick. I sense a très iron fist inside a velvet glove. Speaking of velvet, when are you going to do something about what's inside that black velvet dress young Inocencia wears all the time? She was flirting with you at breakfast again this morning, you know.''

''I wasn't looking. She's not my cup of tea.''

''Merde alors, who are you holding out for, Ellen Terry or the Jersey Lilly? The girl is très belle, and she has no lover. I asked.''

Captain Gringo didn't tell him how wrong he was. He didn't want a dirty old man jerking off in his room while he was trying not to.

A kid was coming down the walk toward them. He slowed warily when he spotted their uniforms. But Gaston called him over and said, ''Tell me, chico, how does a man get laid in this town?''

The kid gulped and replied, ''I am sure my sister is willing, Señor Jurado. But in truth she is ugly, and still a virgin.''

Gaston laughed and said, ''Perhaps a more experienced woman of the town would be more practique. I meant I was looking for a house of ill repute.''

The kid looked relieved and gave them an address down the quay. Then he ran like hell. Not asking for the usual tip. Gaston shrugged and said, ''They certainly make one feel welcome here. Are you coming, my choosy spoiled child?''

''No, thanks. It's no fun with a dame scared out of her wits.''

''Speak for yourself. Many women enjoy being dominated. I'll meet you up at the ogre's castle after la siesta, hein?''

He was wrong. A couple of the uniformed jurado bodyguards tore around the corner, rifles at port arms, and ran up to them. They popped to attention and presented arms as one said, ''You are wanted up at the fortress, señores! They sent us for to search for you!''

Captain Gringo nodded and said, ''You found us. What's up?''

"Some scouts just came in from the jungle, Captain Gringo. They report a column of Colombian soldados coming this way muy pronto!"

Actually, the government column was about a day's march away, if the situation map in El Criado Publico's office meant anything. The scouts and some of the other officers were there with the rebel leader himself, of course, so it was kind of noisy until Captain Gringo shouted, "At ease, damm it! We're not going to get a handle on the situation if we all talk at once!"

Everyone shut up. So he turned to the leader of the patrol that had spotted the Colombians and said, "Bueno. Let's talk about numbers and weapons, first. Did you guys take a head count and did you see any heavy weapons?"

The head scout said, "They were strung out along a chicle gatherers' trail for at least a few hundred meters, Captain Gringo. We could not count them all because we did not see them all. I was watching from up in a tree. I slid down it before any of their own scouts could spot me. I can tell you a full company of infantry is in the lead. Behind them came a train of mules with most unusual packs. Each mule had what looked like a wagon wheel hanging on either side. I could not see what was covered with canvas between the wheels. There were about a dozen such mules. Then others, packing what seemed to be simply big boxes. When I saw more infantry coming along behind the mule train, I thought it wise to get out of there."

One of the young jurados said, "Coward! You should have waited until you'd seen everything!"

Captain Gringo said, "At ease. Scouts aren't supposed to

be brave. They're supposed to get back alive after they make contact with the enemy. Dead scouts tell no tales. So these guys did right.''

He turned to Gaston with a raised eyebrow. The little Frenchman nodded and said, ''Oui, small jungle-artillery pieces. Probably howitzers like we are supposed to have and don't. Short range. Big bang. If they have as many as a dozen, these old Spanish walls won't last too long.''

El Criado Publico said, ''We must do the best we can with what we have. If only we can hold the fort until la *Nombre Nada* returns with our own cannon . . .''

''We can't,'' Captain Gringo cut in, adding, ''No offense, El Criado, but you're a lawyer and I'm the professional soldier you hired. I don't have time for a lecture. So just take my word for it that the guys at the Alamo made a basic blunder that Houston corrected in the open field a few weeks later. The reason we don't build castles anymore is that they went out when cannon were invented.''

''But surely this fort was designed to take some cannon fire, no?''

''The operative word is *some*, El Criado. There's supposed to be at least one big one mounted on each of your six points, and we don't have shit.''

''But with all our rifles and your machine guns, surely we can stop any charge up the steep slopes all around, no?''

''Now why in the hell would anyone order that? They don't have to assault us that way. So they won't. Santa Anna was a jerk-off at the Alamo. He should have dug his infantry in all around, outside Davy Crockett's rifle range, and simply pounded the 'dobe walls flat with his Napoleons. Instead, he made a legend out of a bunch of untrained civilians. The officers leading that Colombian column figure to be a bit smarter than a self-taught Mexican general. They'll be lobbing H.E. shells too, and we don't have anything to lob back."

He turned again to Gaston and asked, "How long do you figure your smith will take, and what sort of range are we talking about?"

Gaston said, "Assuming he's a genius working through the night, he could have a crude but respectable gun for me by about this time mañana. As to range, don't be silly. Three miles is too much to hope for, with a smooth bore and a loose fit."

Captain Gringo said, "I wish you wouldn't say things like that. Okay, you stay here and do the best you can, Gaston. I'll lead a big combat patrol out and we shall see what we shall see."

One of the jurados asked what good Gaston would be here at the fort if his cannon wasn't much good. Captain Gringo said, "You're going to need somebody to lead you through the jungle to the Costa Rican border if I don't make it back."

El Criado Publico gasped and said, "Never! I do not intend to give up without a fight, Captain Gringo!"

The tall American shrugged and said, "Okay. Gaston can lead the smart guys out, then. We haven't got time to talk about it."

With Gaston's help, Captain Gringo had thrown together a hundred picked riflemen and four good machine-gun crews. So for a change he didn't have to pack his own Maxim as he led them through the jungle. He'd taken along noncoms whom Gaston had said were better than average and left behind the natty jurado officers who'd volunteered. This was hardly the time for on-the-job training.

Captain Gringo had the same scouts who'd spotted the approaching column out on point. Like the other guerrillas, they were not local natives, but they'd screwed around in the local jungle enough to know the lay of the land by now. So when one ran back to report they'd reached the river crossing he'd pointed out on the map, he told his followers to take cover as he moved forward to see for himself.

On the map the sluggish little river was a blue line. In real life it was an open slow expanse of tea-colored water about a pistol shot across. He sent a runner for Hernando, the senior noncom he'd picked as segundo, hoping he knew what he was doing. When the mestizo joined him, Captain Gringo said, "We form one firing line here on this side with two-thirds of the men. Each rifleman prone and firing from cover at two-meter intervals. Put Garcia's machine-gun crew upstream. Have Morales and his crew for the other crossbar of the X down on your left flank. Any questions?"

"Sí, Captain Gringo. Who shall give the order to fire?"

"You will, Hernando. Let them make it two-thirds of the way over and then fire at will and make sure Will goes down. Your riflemen will drop most of the guys on your side of the machine-gun crossfire. Anyone retreating back through it will be in lots of trouble. As soon as you drive them back to the cover on the other side, get yourself and your men the hell out of here. Lead them all back to the fort and report to Lieutenant Verrier for further orders."

The burly Hernando frowned and said, "Forgive me, I do not understand those orders, Captain Gringo. I feel certain we can stop them more than one time, no?"

"No. Trained troops don't walk into an ambush twice. Once you've bloodied them, they'll dig in on the far side and start smoking up this position from cover, as they call artillery down on it. But if nobody's home, nobody can get hurt, and meanwhile you'll have delayed their advance at least an hour or so. They won't try another crossing until they've made sure you've retreated. Since they won't know how far you've retreated, they'll move a lot slower from here on, see?"

Hernando brightened and replied, "By the balls of Cristo, I *do*! Hey, I like the way you make war, Captain Gringo. In Mexico our officers kept trying for to get us to die for our cause."

"Don't tell anybody, but that's not professional. The idea is to make the other son of a bitch die for *his* cause. Get moving, muchacho. I have to take my own people over the river and through the woods before grandmother gets here."

He whistled up another guerrilla named Pablo and said, "Your guys and the two other machine guns are moving on. What are you waiting for?"

Then he nodded to a nearby scout and started wading across the shallow and hopefully gator-free river without looking back. He followed the trail a mile and then looked back, and when he saw that Pablo, a rifle platoon, and two machine-gun crews were still with him, told one of the scouts to move down a couple of miles and keep him posted. Then he started to set up his own ambush.

He put most of his men in line flanking the trail from cover, again with a machine-gun nest secured by sharpshooters at each end. He made sure each man had the same orders regarding targets. Then he moved across the trail with the handful of good shots he'd picked as tree snipers. As he sent each one up a tree he told them the same thing: "Remember to stay the hell up there until I personally order you down or, if this doesn't work, until after dark. You've got smokeless powder. But don't fire at anyone looking your way, anyway. The idea is to make them think they're in a cross fire, so they don't complicate our lives by running this way from the main fire line. I want 'em squeezed back down the trail like a tube of toothpaste. If anybody shoots a mule, guess who gets to carry its load?''

They all uaid they understood as he sent them up in the trees to play monkey where they wouldn't be hit by friendly fire coming across the trail to their side.

He went back to his main body and moved down the line once again to make sure every man was well placed. Then he joined the machine-gun crew nearest the approaching enemy column. He didn't want to make the gunner he'd assigned to the Maxim feel unworthy of his confidence. So he sat on a log nearby and chewed an unlit claro, resisting the impulse to repeat his orders about holding fire no matter how tempting a target might be passing in review.

A million years went by before a scout ran breathlessly up the trail to tell him the Colombians were coming. Another million years went by. A parrot shit on the bill of his cap as the jungle came back to life now that he and his men had played dead so long.

And then at last a point scout came up the trail, rifle at port as he moved cautiously and probably feeling very lonely. He swept the thick jungle growth on either side as he scouted ahead of the column. But of course he didn't spot anything. Captain Gringo had promised to bust the ass of anyone who blew it.

The point man moved on out of sight. The parrots went back to crapping and cussing above the once-more-deserted trail. Captain Gringo knew Hernando would let the scout cross the river unmolested before they knifed him quietly, so he forgot about him.

He resisted the impulse to check his watch as they waited. So it only seemed like an hour or so before the main column came up the trail, yakking away and paying even less attention to their surroundings. They had a man on point to worry about it.

The young guerrilla behind the Maxim sucked in his breath as the infantry passed, two abreast. Captain Gringo nudged him with a warning foot and the machine gunner nodded. He was going to be okay.

The guerrilla scouts had been right about it being a full company of infantry in the lead. There was a modest interval, and then the mule train came up the trail. The scouts had been right about the dismounted howitzers. They looked like four-pounders, too. As the first mule packing ammo passed, Captain Gringo read the lettering stenciled on the ammo crate and saw that he was right. Woodbine Arms, Ltd., sold stuff to anybody with money.

Supply mules came behind the light artillery, followed by more infantry. Someone in Panama City was taking El Criado Publico seriously indeed.

He spotted officers passing with the others, but nobody with a higher rank than captain. He didn't know just what this Colonel Maldonado looked like, yet. The last time they'd tangled, Maldonado had played chess at a distance, too. But the son of a bitch was good, and field-grade officers weren't supposed to get themselves killed in the field. Captain Gringo hoped that this time his nibs would be a little closer when the shooting started. Maldonado made him nervous. And if they could pick off somebody who really knew what he was doing, the others figured to be easier to deal with.

Captain Gringo had no way of knowing, of course, that well to the rear, Colonel Maldonado was pissed off about things he found more important than a handful of unwashed gringo-backed guerrillas. Maldonado was in the doghouse again. He'd made it as high as chief of Colombian military intelligence before that last power shift in the Colombian junta. So he really wasn't enjoying this shit detail the winners had handed him. But a good soldado carried out his orders to the letter, and his orders were to wipe out los jurados to the last man, and any women left over.

But the two professionals were not fated to meet that adternoon. By this time the point man had been taken out, and the advance was two-thirds across the ford when Hernando's party opened up on them. When Captain Gringo heard the distant crackle of small-arms fire, he drew his pistol, chose a Colombian officer as his target, and put a .38 slug in his ear.

Then all hell broke loose.

The infantry on the trail before Captain Gringo's ambush started for the cover on the far side and took well-aimed fire from that side, too. Then the survivors headed for home, shooting blindly as they ran back along the trail through flanking fire. The kid behind the Maxim drew a trip wire of death across the trail and the pile-up was awesome until a lucky blind shot silenced him forever, and silenced the machine gun for as long as it took Captain Gringo to shove his corpse out of the way and get behind it.

Everyone on both sides was using smokeless powder. But smokeless was a relative term. So the air was turning blue and hazy as he fired a long burst into now-dim running figures and called out, "Another belt, pronto!" to his ammo man. There was no answer. As the Maxim choked on the end of the spent belt, he turned to see the ammo handler flat on his back, staring up at the tree canopy with a silly grin on his face and a sticky red worm of blood crawling along his hairline.

Another bullet hummed like a bee in Captain Gringo's ear and he knew it hadn't been a lucky shot. Some son of a bitch had his position spotted and was firing from cover on the far side of the trail.

He armed his weapon with another belt and jerked it off its mount to crab sideways with it, shooting from the hip as he got behind a tree. Something solid thunked into the far side of the tree. He doubted it was Paul Bunyan's ax. He took off his hat and skimmed it away. He spotted the muzzle flash across the trail this time as his tormentor fired at it by reflex. He nodded grimly, took a deep breath, and swung the machine-gun muzzle around the far side of the tree to blow the wise-ass and the bushes he was hidden by to red and green confetti. Then he went to get another ammo belt. Nobody seemed to want to argue about it.

But by now there was nothing left to shoot at. Nothing moving, in any case. Some of the bodies sprawled on the trail by the score had been hit a dozen times by now. So he called out, "Cease fire!"

They did. Pablo ran over to him, grinning like a mean little kid, to salute and ask what happened next. Captain Gringo said, "Move two squads up the trail to secure those pack mules. Get 'em off the trail and under cover on the double."

"Sí, sí. What about the men leading them?"

"What the fuck do we want with *them*? Get moving, muchacho!"

Pablo did. Captain Gringo whistled in some other noncoms and told them, "Move your people back from the trail. I'm expecting incoming mail."

"What about our own dead and wounded, Captain Gringo?"

"We carry our wounded. Colombia can bury, stuff, or do

whatever they like with our dead. Let's get our *living* the hell out of here, before they buy it, too!"

A giant tore canvas across the sky above, and as the first shell hit, short and wide, he added, "See what I mean? Vamanos, muchachos! It's time to get our asses and those mules someplace that's not so noisy!"

They didn't make it back to the fort with all the mules and field guns, and they'd left eleven good men behind, too. But as they staggered through the fortress gates well after sundown they still had the four Maxims, seven four-pound howitzers, and enough ammo to matter. Gaston said the hitherto-useless shells Esperanza had delivered would fit the captured weapons as well. So things were looking up.

As Gaston supervised setting up a howitzer on each point of the star fort, with the one leftover aimed at max elevation from the center of the parade, a council of war was held in Zagal's office.

El Criado Publico and his young squirts seemed to think the war was over and that they'd won. Captain Gringo warned, "It's just getting a little harder for the other side, El Criado. I didn't get to shoot any bird colonels this afternoon. So old Maldonado and his guys are holding a meeting just like this one, about now. Maldonado's good, and he can count. He knows now we've got the same kind of guns as he has, and he'd be a real dope if he hasn't got this old Spanish fort well detailed on his own situation map."

A junior jurado laughed and said, "He must know it would be sheer suicide to attack us now. I'll bet they don't stop running all the way back to Panama City! The muchachos tell me the river crossing ran red with their blood to the sea, and you must have killed a whole company along the trail, no?''

''More like a couple of platoons,'' Captain Gringo replied, explaining, ''You'd be surprised how few dead bodies it takes to look like a wiped-out brigade. It doesn't take more than a dozen cancan girls to spread across a whole stage and make it look like every girl in Paris is showing you her crotch at once. Meanwhile, trained troops can accept up to about a one-third loss before their officers can't keep them from retreating. We sure didn't wipe out anything like a third of Maldonado's column, and he's got 'em trained pretty good.''

Another jurado said, ''Let them come, then. We can handle them.''

Captain Gringo said, ''They'll be coming. The second idea is still up for grabs.''

''What do you suggest?'' El Criado Publico asked gravely.

The tall American repressed a yawn and said, ''We'd better eat and get some sleep, for openers. I'd say our ambush bought us at least another forty-eight hours. If I was wearing Colonel Maldonado's boots I'd bury my dead, make camp, and send for replacements and heavier artillery before I did much more.''

Another uniformed tyro asked, ''For why does he need more guns? You just said you only captured a few of his weapons, Captain Gringo.''

The American said, ''Maldonado knows exactly how many of his four-pounders we captured. He knows we're dug in on higher ground, too. So Gaston would have the range on him in an artillery duel, and Gaston's good. Unless that Colombian colonel's an idiot, and I don't think he is, he won't move into artillery range until he has longer-range artillery. The advantage the attacker always has in these dumb Alamo situations is that his lines of supply remain open and he can move in or move back whenever he damn pleases."

He looked at the situation map, nodded, and added, "Okay, the nearest railroad's so far we can forget it, and the nearest decent port to land heavy stuff figures to be San Cristobal, a hundred miles by crow, and a crow can't carry a siege gun. If they could get gunboats in across the shallow lagoon to our northeast, they'd have done so by now and wouldn't be fucking around in the jungle. So, yeah, maybe more than forty-eight hours. Then we could be in big trouble."

On that note the meeting broke up and they all went to dinner.

Some of them did, at any rate. Gaston was still working to set up the guns and Inocencia hadn't come to the table when Captain Gringo arrived after washing up. He found Bowman and the redhead across from him tonight.

The other American looked sort of green around the gills and Martha Pendergast seemed a little tense about something. He didn't worry about it. It was probably either a lover's quarrel or maybe not enough loving at all. They both toyed with their food as their host pontificated at the head of the table about defending the fort to the last drop of his blue blood. The other jurados looked a bit more dubious about spilling their own. But he could probably depend on them sticking around at least until somebody got hurt.

The food, as usual, was good and more than ample. As long as the old man wanted to talk about siege warfare, Captain Gringo suggested it might be a good idea to cut the rations in half, at least, saying, "The first thing Maldonado's going to try will be to cut us off from the village and surrounding farms. We're okay for water, thanks to the nice deep wells the old Spanish engineers drilled down through this rise. But we could wind up on short rations before te gives up for the rainy season, if he does, and these long stuffy meals use up a lot of grub."

El Criado Publico shrugged and said, "My people and I are used to dining in the high-born Spanish fashion, and in any case we have supplies on hand to last us indefinitely."

Captain Gringo insisted, "That Colombian strike forced headed our way could have indefinite plans about *leaving*, too, sir. I keep saying it, but nobody seems to want to listen. You don't overthrow a government by letting it besiege you in a fixed position!"

The silver-haired El Criado Publico said, "I am open to suggestions, if you know a better way, Captain Gringo."

So the American swallowed the coffee in his mouth and said, "Any way would be better than trying to fight from fixed positions. As I see it, you're in much the same position as Washington was at the beginning of a revolution that worked, except that Washington had a lot bigger army. He kept it moving around, never letting the British box him where they might have wiped him out with their superior arms and trained regulars. The Continental Congress wanted him to hold New York to the last man. But he retreated to White Plains anyway. He knew that once he let himself be surrounded it would all be over. The British took New York. So what? There was no last drop of rebel blood to be spilled there. So they had to chase him to Philly. He let 'em take Philly, too. Again, so what? The redcoats were out to capture the Continental army, not real estate."

One of the junior officers frowned across at him and said, "I thought your great Washington won by simply beating the British, Captain Gringo."

The ex-West Pointer shook his head and said with a wry smile, "That may be the way they teach it in the history books today. But in point of fact Washington *lost* most of the time. He'd have lost *every* time if a couple of British generals hadn't been awfully stupid. The point is that he lost lots on battles and won the war.''

The redhead across the table asked, ''How on earth could he have done that, Dick? You don't sound very patriotic!''

Her escort growled, ''He's not patriotic. He's a renegade. He's full of bull, too. Everybody knows Washington was a great general!''

Captain Gringo smiled pleasantly at Bowman and said, ''That's what I just said. Washington won because he kept his Continental army in the field for eight long years by refusing to play the game the way the redcoats wanted him to. In the end the Brits gave up, not because they'd been beaten, but because the war was expensive and figured to go on forever. The situation here is similar. We don't have to burn down Bogotá to beat Colombia. We just have to convince them Panama's not worth the time and trouble.''

The older man at the head of the table nodded sagely and said, ''In that case, what are we arguing about? As I said, we can hold here until hell freezes over!''

Captain Gringo shook his head and said, ''Even if we could, so what? What would it cost the Colombian junta to keep you bottled up in one small corner of the isthmus while they go right on running and collecting taxes from the rest of it? If I was running your revolution I'd start by evacuating this backwoods fort and making them *work* at fighting us! I'd move closer to Panama City, where people read newspapers, and hit and run until guys who were tired of the dictatorship came out to join us. Can't you see Bogotá doesn't really care what a few simple fisherfolk out in the middle of nowhere do or say? Hell, there's only one railroad running across the isthmus. A handful of guerrillas could cripple the economy, and you have *more* than a handful, El Criado!''

The older man shook his head and said, "Unthinkable. I did not come down here for to be a bandit leader. I have already begun my social reforms here. I need the port for to receive more supplies from my backers in los Estados Unidos."

Captain Gringo shrugged, swallowed more coffee, and suggested, "Let me take a couple of hundred guys out for some distracting tactics, then. If we were to raise some hell in other parts, Maldonado might chase us instead of besieging you here, see?"

The rebel leader asked Bowman what he thought of the idea, as if Bowman knew. The liaison man shrugged and said, "It sounds like Jesse James to me. But that comes as no great surprise, from a Jesse James."

"Up yours, too," Captain Gringo said, sweetly.

El Criado Publico said, "We shall discuss diversionary tactics at a more convenient time. After we repel the current assault."

Captain Gringo said, "El Criado, once Maldonado has us boxed, there ain't gonna *be* no diversionary nothing! You know how the Continental army won its only two important victories? At both Saratoga and Yorktown the redcoats took up siege positions and let us Yanks pound them until they had to give up. Every time they fought us in the *field*, they won!"

The redhead said, "My Jim is right! You're just horrid to speak that way about the father of our country, Dick Walker!"

That was too dumb to answer. So he didn't try. Inocencia Zagal came in, wearing a pout and a puzzled frown as well as black vlvet. She took her seat, saying, "I can't find my pet, Diablo, anywhere. How could he have gotten out of the fort? Nobody I asked has seen him since I left him tied up in my room this afternoon when I went down to the village!"

Her father, at the head of the table, said, "I assure you

your cat is safe and well, my pet. I had him locked up down below in the fortress dungeons."

The chestnut-haired beauty gasped and demanded, "For why? How dare you do such a thing without consulting me, father!"

Her father said soothingly, "You were not here. I did it not for to annoy either you or that dangerous animal, Inocencia. We may be under fire here at any moment, and one can hardly have a wild jungle cat running loose at such times, eh?"

"But, father, I have Diablo under perfect control, I assure you!"

"That may be so, Inocencia. But have you ever tried to control that powerful jaguar amid falling debris, or with the smell of blood in the air? Be reasonable, child. I know you love your pet, as he no doubt loves you. But he is nevertheless a large, dangerous beast. I have seen domesticated farm animals turn on their owners when startled by a loud noise or, heaven forbid, pain. The jaguar stays down in the dungeons, where he can neither be harmed or harm anyone, until after this emergency ends."

He sounded like he meant it. Inocencia got up and flounced out of the room as Martha Pendergast murmured, "Poor thing. She seems so fond of that big cat, and it's sort of cute, once one gets used to it."

Captain Gringo managed not to laugh. It wasn't easy. As if to change the subject, El Criado Publico said, "We must consider the safety of our civilian citizens, Captain Gringo. We obviously don't have roofed quarters enough for the whole village. But if we let them camp on the parade . . ."

"They'll get wet," Captain Gringo cut in, adding, "The rainy season is starting and, even if it was the dry season, there's just not room out there. They'd be packed like sardines and we'd have half of them down with diarrhea in no time."

Across the table, Bowman gasped, said, "Jesus, Walker!" and got to his feet to bolt from the room. The redhead he'd left behind blushed and said, "Oh, you shouldn't have said that. My Jim has been suffering an upset tummy since we got here."

El Criado Publico sniffed and said, "I agree it is not a topic for dinner conversation. But we must do something about the security of my people."

Captain Gringo nodded and said, "Leave them alone to fend for themselves, then. I don't see why a pro like Maldonado would shell the village down by the water. He and his men won't occupy it until they take this high ground, because we *could*, from up here. He'll dig in along the tree line to the west to cut us off from the jungle."

He took another sip of coffee before he added wearily, "That's if we're dumb enough to let him, of course. There's still plenty of time to move inland and set up flexible lines of defense. Artillery isn't worth much in heavy timber against a shifting target."

The rebel leader frowned and said, "That would mean abandoning the villagers I've just liberated to the mercy of the enemy!"

"So what? Maldonado's a professional soldier, not a butcher. He won't put anyone against the wall unless they shout viva la revolución a lot, and they won't. There are other villages to liberate. The idea is to keep a viable army in the field and make them expend time and money on your movement."

"But I have worked so hard at reforming this particular area."

"Okay. So it's reformed. Once the rains start in earnest, it should be safe to dig in for the season in some other village and reform the hell out of it. That Colombian column will go back to Panama City to dry out, and meanwhile you'll have survived longer than the average rebel movement ever gets to in these parts."

"We are talking in circles, Captain Gringo, and my mind is made up."

That seemed for sure. So when the next course was served, Captain Gringo ate silently and then excused himself from dessert to go see how Gaston was making out.

He found the dapper little Frenchman up on one of the star points, dismissing the crew who had just placed one of the captured howitzers to his taste. The position overlooked the fising village and wide moonlit lagoon to the east. The night was clear and pleasantly cool with the trades picking up again. But the air still held a hint of brass polish. Captain Gringo took a drag on his claro and said, "I sure wish that hurricane out there would swing ashore."

Gaston said, "Oui. It would be très amuse to sit high and dry as our playmates from Panama City flounder about in tangled wet spinach. You just missed another amusing sight, Dick. That strange girl, Inocencia, just asked me to help her get her pussy back. It appears they have locked the creature up somewhere, and Inocencia seems to think I have the rank to restore it to liberty. I told her I found her pussy worthy of my total admiration, but alas, I only work here, non?"

Captain Gringo grimaced and said, "Both her pussies are sort of weird. The old man's locked it up down below. For once he makes sense. *I* sure wouldn't want that thing coming up behind me in the middle of a firefight!"

Gaston said, "Oui. That is what I just told her. Speaking of weird pussy, Dick, have you noticed something weird indeed about the pussy situation here?"

"I just said I had. Inocencia's nuts, and that redhead can't be as dumb as she sounds."

Gaston shook his head and said, "Never mind the pussy that we know and love. What I wish to know is where the *missing* pussy might be!"

"We're missing some dame?"

"We are missing more than one! Until M'mselle Pendergast arrived, no doubt unexpectedly, Inocencia was the only female in this fort! She does not even have the usual duenna required by Spanish custom. There are no female servants. Rank has its privileges in any garrison, but not even the officers have the usual adelitas. Some of th enlisted men have girls down in the village. I asked. But no women are allowed in the barracks up here.I am beginning to suspect we may have enlisted into a bed of pansies!"

Captain Gringo frowned thoughtfully and said, "The old man can't be, if he's a widower with a grown daughter."

"He may have felt confused in his youth. The enlisted rebels come in all shapes and sizes, but have you noticed that every one of his officers is a pretty-boy?"

"Oh, come on. Has anybody tried to get you to bend over for the soap? They do seem young and overzealous. But so would a bunch of monkish students, and we know the old goat was a law professor in Cuba before he decided to put his theories into practice."

Gaston said, "If they are college boys, they must have gone to one très strange school. I was, as you know, raised in the same faith. So when I was forced to go to school at all I naturally attended Catholic school. It is not true that choirboys are sexless."

"So I've heard. Come to think of it, these jurado guys are sort of androgynous. They don't act interested in sex one way or the other."

He thought, and added, "Isn't there a Catholic order that, ah, sort of castrates its monks?"

Gaston blinked in surprise and replied, "Mais non! This is the nineteenth century, not Renaissance Italy! The Popes long ago forbade the creation of castrati choirboys, on pain of excommunication. There is still some obscure Russian sect that cuts off balls for God. But what can one expect from mad Russians, hein?"

Captain Gringo shrugged and said, "I understand more than one Pope tried to stop the Spanish Inquisition, when playing with matches got a little out of hand, too. But did anybody *listen?*"

"True. The Spanish have always considered themselves more Catholic than any mere Pope. But how are we to check your interesting theory? I, for one, am not about to ask any jurado to drop his pants for me. If he were to turn out to be a mundane miraposa, we could both end up feeling très silly!"

Captain Gringo laughed at the mental picture and said, "The guy who's really out to shove it up our tails is somewhere out in the jungle with an army. So let's not worry about the guys on our side, as long as they have the balls to fight."

Gaston said, "I have a better idea. Let's run for Costa Rica and let them fight *alone!* This is not a good situation, Dick. Maldonado knows what he is doing. Zagal does not."

"I know. I just tried to talk sense to him. But we took the money, and I could sure use that presidential pardon!"

"Oui, even though I shall miss you if you go back to Connecticut to be a Yankee. But what good would a full pardon from your President Cleveland do you against a Colombian wall? That is where we shall all wind up unless someone around here begins to think rational thoughts, you know!"

Captain Gringo nodded and replied, "I know. Meanwhile, we've got a day or so to work something out. So I'm turning in. Are you coming?"

"Not yet. You don't need me to jerk you to sleep. I shall stay and admire the view for a while. If la *Nombre Nada* appears on the horizon I shall sleep a lot better. We have to have something to outrange the twin of this adorable howitzer, and if Esperanza brings me a gun with a longer tube, I may stick around awhile."

So Captain Gringo went below to hit the sack. Gaston leaned against the rough stone battlement and gazed out to sea as he smoked his own cigar. He turned when he heard a soft footstep and saw Inocencia standing there in the moonlight. She said, "It is no use. They won't let me see poor Diablo. They said it was my father's order. Oh, how I hate that man!"

Gaston said cautiously, "I make it my practice never to involve my tender nose in family quarrels, señorita. No doubt you feel your father is strict, but I am sure he means well, hein?"

"My father is a monster," Inocencia said flatly. Then she moved in closer and said, "Listen, caballero, if you will help me get Diablo out of that dungeon I will let you fuck me."

Gaston gasped and replied, "Mon Dieu! I am overwhelmed by your offer! But as I told you before, there is nothing I can do about your adorable pussy. The one in the celler, I mean."

"What is the matter, don't you wish for to fuck me?"

As a matter of fact, Gaston had to think about that. In his time, old Gaston had shoved his dong into some pretty ugly stuff, and the girl was really beautiful. But she was also obviously emotionally unstable, and her father owned a private army. He said, with a gallantry he didn't really feel, "It would probably kill me. But I can't think of a better way to die, señorita. On the other hand, there is simply no way for me to get at your other pussy. I am not in command here. Your father is.''

She pouted her lush lower lip and said, ''It's not fair. Father will not let me encourage anyone to pay court to me, and now he has deprived me of my sole companion. I hate to sleep alone.''

Gaston sighed and said, ''One gets used to it by the time one reaches my age. I have always tried to avoid it as much as possible. But that is life, non?''

She regarded him thoughtfully in the moonlight for a time, then she smiled, in an oddly disturbing manner, and said, ''My father would have a fit if I went to bed with a man as old as he.''

''True, señorita. Perhaps we should not tell him, hein?''

Gaston thought she was joking. But Inocencia took his hand and said, ''Bueno. We won't. Come with me, caballero. For I mean to fuck you like a madwoman!''

So, a while later, when Captain Gringo heard noises next door and unplugged the pinhole to see what in the hell was going on in there, he was surprised to see Gaston, of all people, going sloppy seconds to a jaguar. They both seemed to be enjoying it as Gaston humped the lovely young Inocencia dog-style instead of cat-style. For one thing, Gaston had a surprisingly big dong for such a little guy, and the chestnut-haired beauty was arching her spine to take it all as she showed them both how much she admired older men.

Captain Gringo plugged the hole again and got back in bed with his book. It was shitty to play peeping Tom on a buddy, and if they hadn't caught her with the jaguar by this time, Gaston probably wouldn't get caught in there either. Like most overstrict fathers, El Criado Publico probably thought that all one had to do to keep a daughter pure was simply to make sure she didn't go out at night. Captain Gringo chuckled fondly as he remembered that girl down the block back home who was only allowed to speak to young men on her porch swing. She sure had given great blow jobs.

He'd relit the lamp to read and his pants were handy when he heard a soft knock on his own door. So he only had to haul on his pants and pick up his .38 and he was in shape to receive visitors.

It was Martha Pendergast. The redhead blushed when she saw he was bare from the waist up. He didn't see why. She was in her nightgown. And it was a thin one.

She said, "I have to talk to you about my Jim."

He said, "I wish you wouldn't. I'm not a doctor. But I think it's yellow jack. I don't want to know anything else about him."

She came in and shut the door before she insisted, "There's something wrong with him, and I don't mean the trots he seems to have picked up from the water here. Do you find me attractive, Dick?"

"Sure. You've only got one head and I don't see any scars. But I thought you were spoken for, Martha."

She said, "I did, too. But Jim hasn't touched me since we got engaged."

"Well, aside from having the trots, he could be an old-fashioned boy."

She frowned and said, "I'm an old-fashioned girl. But not *that* old-fashioned! Heavens, we're almost in the twentieth century, and, you know, we're supposed to be *engaged!*"

He moved back toward the bed as he chuckled and replied, "I get the picture. Ah, have you been engaged before, Martha?"

"Only a few times. I wouldn't want you to think I was a loose woman."

"Oh, heaven forfend! I understand your problem completely. It would be kind of dumb to marry a guy for keeps without trying him on for size first, wouldn't it?"

"That's exactly what I suggested to my Jim. But he said the idea was shocking. He said he'd promised his dying mother that the girl he would someday marry would be pure."

He sat on the bed, saying, "Well, I won't tell on you, if you still mean to marry the jerk-off."

She sat down beside him as she sighed and said, "I suppose I ought to. Jim has a very good job and I'm almost twenty-five. I'll probably never get a better offer, and I'd hate to die an old maid."

He doubted that was liable to be her fate as he caught a whiff of her perfumed body odor. But he said, "I don't see what you need *me* for, then. I'm not a justice of the peace."

She leaned even closer as she said, "No, but you're a man of the world and I need your advice, Dick. I think I've patched things up after sort of shocking Jim. I cried a little and told him I'd just been testing him. You know how it goes."

"Boy, do I know how it goes. I'm still missing something, Martha. If you mean to go ahead and marry the guy without a physical exam, what can I tell you?"

"How to act like a virgin. As we were making up, I had to tell a few little white lies. You know, his dying mother and all."

Captain Gringo laughed incredulously and asked, "Hell, don't you even *remember* what it feels like to be a virgin?"

"Not really. You see, when I was about nine there was this boy next door and one day as we were playing doctor . . ."

He cut in with another laugh and said, "I'm beginning to see the light. Getting into slap-and-giggle before one's been properly scared by Queen Victoria could make it tough to play the blushing bride, I suppose. But, hell, how experienced could Jim Bowman be, if he talks so dumb? Just tell him you ride bikes a lot, and cry a little on your wedding night, and he'll probably buy your tales of innocence."

"I'd already thought of how I cried when I hit that bump on a hard bicycle seat, Dick. But I'm worried just the same. As were making up, Jim confessed he'd been wicked a few times as a student at Yale."

"He went to Yale? That explains a lot."

"He said he'd been to a house of ill repute more than once. But that he's reformed and very ashamed of his misspent youth. I forgave him for not being a virgin. I don't think he'd be as broad-minded if he suspected *I* might not be."

"I think you're right. But what do you expect me to do about it, audition you as a virgin?"

She clapped her hand's and said, "Oh, would you?"

He told her he'd be glad to as she pulled her nightgown off over her red head and lay back stark naked and redheaded all over.

He shucked his pants and didn't bother with the lamp as he got right down to testing her virgin act. It wasn't very convincing. As he mounted her she hissed in pleasure, bit down with her internal muscles, and came up to meet him in a series of most experienced bumps and grinds. He grinned down at her in the lamplight and said, "Take it easy, Red. You're not supposed to come, the first night."

"Oh, pooh, that hardly seems fair. Kiss me and *help* me come, you big silly."

So he did. Her French kissing was another mistake, but he enjoyed it, so what the hell. Martha spread her creamy thighs wider to take him deeper as she dug her nails into his buttocks to take it all the way. She moaned, "Oh, I like to feel it touch bottom with every stroke like that. I hope my Jim has a cock as big as yours, dear.''

He grimaced in distaste and kissed her lush lips again to keep her from talking so dumb. They were both hard up, so they came soon, together.

As they paused for breath, she giggled and said, ''That felt marvelous. I wish *we* could be engaged for a while. Did it feel like you were fucking a virgin, dear?''

''Hardly. I don't think even a Yale man would buy your hot tamale as a cherry pie. Can't you even *act* like you're not sure you want to?''

She raised her knees, locked her ankles across his bare rump, and said, ''But I *do* want to, Dick. Doesn't *everybody* like to fuck?''

''Hmmm. I can see I'm going to have to calm you down a bit before we consider the finer points of wedding-night dramatics.''

''Oh, goody! Let me get on top this time!''

He did. The view was inspiring as she moved her creamy body and red pubic thatch up and down, her head thrown back as her perky white breasts bobbed with lives of their own to follow. He hadn't had any woman at all for some time, and the redhead was better than most. But, for a virgin, old Martha sure was acrobatic.

She stopped halfway to heaven and said conversationally, ''I want to try something my second or third beau taught me when we got engaged. He wasn't nearly as big as you.''

He didn't answer as she wedged her naked legs around and got a bare heel planted in each of his armpits, bracing herself on locked elbows with her hands gripping his shins when she leaned farther back and said, in that same dumb baby-doll voice, ''Tickle me while I go up and down, dear.''

He grinned and reached down to place his palm against her

soft lower belly, with his thumb on her clit as he rotated it in the moisture where her red pubic hair parted pinkly. She hissed in pleasure and began to move up and down with his more vital organ clasped tightly inside her. She asked, "Isn't this nice?" and he responded by coming in her, hard. She giggled when she felt it and kept moving. He didn't mind at all. So by the time she'd climaxed that way, he was fully aroused again, and since she seemed to enjoy acrobatics, they wound up in some very odd positions indeed before she finally said, "Seriously, Dick. I want you to give me some fucking lessons."

He laughed like hell, since he was pounding her from above and behind pretty good when she said it. But he knew what she meant. So he withdrew, rolled her over on her back again, and said, "Okay. Pretend this is your wedding night and we just got into bed."

"But, Dick, I'm not going to marry *you*. I'm going to marry Jim."

"Whatever. The first thing you do is cross your legs and tell me to stop and let you think about the awful things I seem to be about to do to you."

"Like this?"

"Yeah. Now I'll lie down beside you and we'll skip the crap about how I'd never hurt you for the world and only want to make you mine. You flinch and bite your lower lip when I put my hand between your legs like this and . . . damm it, Martha, that's not flinching. You're supposed to keep your legs *together*!"

"Pooh. How are you going to make me yours if I don't spread my legs?"

"*I'm* supposed to worry about that. Okay. You keep your legs together and, ah, tremble when I kiss you and then kiss your nipple like this and . . . Don't shove it up to me, damm it. You're supposed to be shocked. Nobody's ever touched your tits before, see?''

That struck her funny and she laughed like hell. He laughed, too. Then he said, "Okay, let's try another approach."

"Goody. You haven't eaten my pussy yet."

"I'm not about to, either, on your wedding night. Let's try it this way. Pretend I'm ugly and covered with running sores and that you don't want to let me because I'll probably give you a dose."

"Ooh, how icky!"

"Hey, that's a great expression. Practice it. Okay. I'm trying to lay you and you don't want me to. It's awful. You're a beautiful princess being raped by an ogre, see?"

It worked, up to a point. The redhead enjoyed sex games and she was reasonably convincing as she tried to shove him back with her soft palms, rolling her head from side to side on the pillow with her eyes closed as she pleaded, "No, no, a thousand times no! I'd rather die than say yes." But then she blew it, when, as he forced her thighs apart and fumbled his ogre's ugly dong into position, she added, "Wheeee!" and came up to take him damn near balls and all.

So he gave up and just enjoyed her for a while. He was wondering if she meant to spend the whole night with him, and what he'd tell Gaston when and if the Frenchman came in from next door. But the redhead solved the problem by saying, as they were doing it dog-style, "I really have to get back to my own quarters, Dicky wicky."

"Do you have to go right now?"

"No. Let's come again before I go."

Meanwhile, in the room next door, Gaston had put Inocencia to sleep with his own lovemaking and was sitting up in bed, smoking, when he noticed the place on the wall where a coral block had fallen out. Knowing he was in a rather delicate position, and having encountered walls with ears before, Gaston got up quietly to investigate. He took along the oil lamp and some matches in case it should go out.

He held the light up to the gap and peered in. He saw the gleam of wet soap where wet soap should not have been. He frowned and poked the plug out with a match stem. Then, seeing light on the other side, he blew out the lamp on his side before peeking through the pinhole.

Then he grinned with relief. No jurado had been spying on him and El Criado Publico's daughter. His young friend, Captain Gringo, had made friends with the redhead after all. He watched them going dog-style for a time. Then he decided a gentleman didn't take such naughty liberties with a friend and turned away, murmuring, "Bless you, my children," as he relit the lamp.

On the red satin bedspread, the sulty Inocencia opened her eyes dreamily and asked why he was out of bed. Gaston rejoined her, saying, "I was merely stretching my poor old legs, ma chere."

Inocencia spread her own, sensuously, as she murmured, "Come back to bed, querido. You are not as old as I took you for, where it matters."

He did, of course, but as he remounted the stunningly beautiful girl he asked, "Is it safe for me to stay much longer?"

She said, simply, "Sí, my father has not once come to sleep with me since he began this silly nonsense about reforming the world."

At the breakfast table, neither Inocencia nor the redhead acted like they had done anything in bed the night before more interesting than saying their prayers. So neither soldier of fortune more than smiled politely as they said good morning, ate, and got the hell out of there.

Gaston asked Captain Gringo to go with him when he checked out the blacksmith. As they walked down the slope together, Gaston said, "I have something to tell you about the très strange morality of this new republic, Dick. To be begin with, I spent most of the night with Inocencia."

"I heard you creeping in the wee small hours."

"Eh bien, I waited until your redhead left, to be discreet. Our great leader's daughter tells a strange tale about her childhood, Dick."

"Did she tell you she's been screwing that jaguar?"

"Ah, that accounts for the smell, and I see it was you who plugged that pinhole with soap. Beastiality is only one of her problems, although it doubtless explains why her strange pet seems so devoted to her. She told me her father began having sex with her right after her mother died, when she was eight years old."

"Oh boy, and you believed her? The mixed-up little dame obviously hates her father, and what does a dame always say about a guy she hates?"

Gaston shrugged and said, "We have all heard rape fantasies, of course. But hers are rather unusual. For one thing, she says she *enjoyed* sex with her own father. She said until he got a bit on in years and began to take more interest in politics than her rather formidable body, she sincerely loved him and desired no other man but him. They both read more than might be good for them, and he told her, when he broke her in as a child, that according to some German philosopher, superior people like them were above the mundane morality of lesser mortals. It sounds like a German. I told you how they fired on our truce flag back in Seventy; non?"

Captain Gringo grimaced and said, "I read the book Zagal wrote, too. He seems pretty letter-of-the-law for a superman who molests little girls."

"Merde alors, every ruler expects his subjects to behave. In merry England they lock up common working men for molesting an adult woman on the streets. But the Prince of Wales is still living openly with more than one married woman, and I still think Jack the Ripper was Prime Minister Gladstone."

"I thought he was the Duke of Clarence. Getting back to the local first family, Inocencia is weird for sure. If her old man's a reformed baby raper, what do you expect *me* to do about it? If you had the brains of a gnat you'd stay the hell away from her."

Gaston said he had the brains of a gnat but the cock of a man, and pointed out that Jim Bowman could mess them up pretty good, too, if he found out about Captain Gringo and the redhead. He added, "The most pratique solution, should Esperanza get back before we are all killed by the Colombian army, would be to board the *Nombre Nada*, with or without the girls, and sail almost anywhere else, hein?"

Captain Gringo didn't answer. It sure was boring to hear everybody play the same gramaphone records, over and over around here.

At the smithy, they found Gaston's crude cannon finished before the promised time. The blacksmith looked it. He was covered with cuts and burns as well as sweat when he showed it to them and pleaded, "You will tell our great liberator I did my very best, no?"

Gaston said he sure would. Captain Gringo asked, "Why are you so worried, amigo? Don't you enjoy being liberated?"

The smith made the sign of the cross and replied, "Oh, very very much, I assure you. I agree it is only just what the punishment should fit the crime. Es verdad, I believed this long before El Criado came for to put things in perfect order here."

Gaston asked about the gun carriage he'd sketched. The smith said the shipwright would have it finished soon and offered to go fetch him. Running. Gaston said not to bother, but to have someone wheel the whole mess up to the fort when it was ready. He asked how much they owed. The smith looked like he was about to burst into tears as he replied, "Es por nada, I assure you, señores! It was an honor to have been of service to the new government. It would be wrong to take payment for serving one's country, no?"

Captain Gringo took out some money and put it on the anvil, saying, "Don't be an idiot. Not even der Kaiser gets his cannon from Krupp por nada."

The smith stared down at the money as if it were a cobra coiled to strike, and gasped, and, "For the love of God, don't try to get me in trouble, señores! I did as you asked, no? For why do you wish to see me taken to the pits of justice? You do not have to test me with temptation. I have not asked for dinero. Look, I am not *touching* the dinero, see?"

Captain Gringo muttered, "Waste not, want not," and put the money away.

The smith fell to his knees in sick relief, eyes closed in silent prayer.

Outside, Captain Gringo growled, "Okay, so what's a pit of justice?"

"Merde alors, how should I know? It sounds like something I, for one, do not wish to fall into! Perhaps if we asked at the cantina . . ."

"Skip it. I'm tired of seeing probrecitos piss their pants every time I talk to them wearing this uniform. Are you sure we're fighting for the good guys this time, Gaston?"

"We know the Colombian junta are bad guys indeed. I shall have to ask Inocencia about these pits of whatever. I think they have her pet jaguar in at least one of them. Apparently our host is holding other prisoners in the old fortress dungeons."

"That smith back there didn't act like he was just worried about going to jail, and Zagal admires the Spanish Inquisition."

They'd moved up the slope a way by now. So Captain Gringo turned and swept the seaward horizon with his eyes as Gaston said, "Great minds run in the same channels, I see. But I do not see the black sail of la *Nombre Nada* out there, alas."

"Yeah, we've got to hang around at least until she gets back. I'd hate like hell to risk an overland running gunfight with a guerrilla army we just trained pretty good. I don't want Esperanza sailing in blind if anyone here is mad at her pals, either. Let's just go on back up and play her by ear some more. Inocencia's hopefully just nuts and that smith could just be stupid."

They had the crude but impressive wrought-iron cannon in position on the parade by that afternoon. It was chambered for the same four-pound rounds as the howitzers on both sides. Gaston said that with the tube elevated to forty-five degrees it might have a little more range than a howitzer, despite its smooth bore. Accuracy, of course, was too much even to dream of.

Near sundown one of the scouts Captain Gringo had ordered out to patrol came in with dismal news. Unless the scout was nuts or the map was wrong, the Colombian column had pushed in closer than Captain Gringo had expected until they got some big guns of their own. The scout showed them where the Colombians were bivouacked in the jungle to the southwest and said they hadn't set up their own howitzers when he'd lit out.

Gaston nodded at the map and said, "Oui, they are just out of range for the howitzers they know we have, even with our superior altitude. Naturally, they can't suspect I, the best artilleryman in all of Latin America, have a longer tube as well as higher ground to play with, hein?"

Captain Gringo said, "They're way out of range, genius."

Gaston said, "Thank you. I am. If I wrap the projectile in greased rawhide for a smoother fit, then fire it with a surcharge of loose powder from some of the other rounds we have to spare . . ."

"Gaston, you're loco en la cabeza!" Captain Gringo cut in, adding for the others in the room who might not have been out in the hot sun so long, "That cobbled-together hunk of junk wouldn't be safe with a fixed round. Double charge her and she'll split open like an overripe banana!"

Gaston shrugged and said, "It would take at least a *triple* charge to reach those map coordinates, Dick. Naturally I intend to use a long lanyard, and we had better make sure all the windows facing inward are open. It will be très noisy no matter what happens, hein?"

Gaston studied the map again, memorized the figures, and marched out, muttering, "Soup of the duck."

El Criado Publico looked at Captain Gringo and asked nervously, "Do you think he knows what he is doing?"

The American said, "No. But we have to do something, and we just can't shake 'em up from here with the howitzers."

So they let Gaston try.

It took him twenty minutes and a lot of cursing before he and his improvised weapon loaded and aimed. Then he ordered his gun crew to run for cover as he backed away, unreeling a long length of rawhide riata attached to the sort of mousetrap firing mechanism he'd devised.

As everyone watched from a safer distance, Gaston got behind the pile of sandbags he'd had them build for him a hundred fifty feet away. Then he pulled.

The resultant roar was deafening and the whole hill trembled as the triple charge hurled the patched shell skyward and, for some strange reason, failed to burst the breech or the tube.

Gaston stepped into view again as everyone cheered, took off his cap, and bowed. Then he got back to work recharging for a second round.

Far out in the jungle, bedded down for the night, well out of howitzer range, Colonel Maldonado was writing at the folding field desk in his tent when he heard something he knew he shouldn't be hearing and looked up with a puzzled frown.

Gaston's big gun was wildly inaccurate to begin with and he was firing blind in any case. It still worried Colonel Maldonado when the first shell screamed down ass-over-teakettle, hit short and wide of the camp with an audible thud, then exploded when its time-fuse went off.

Maldonado ran outside and shouted, "Douse those damned campfires!" as an aide ran up to him while everyone else ran around like the ants of a stepped-on nest. The aide saluted and said, "We seem to be under fire, sir."

Maldonado grimaced and said, "Tell me about it. That report from our field agent in Limón was right. Nobody but that damned Captain Gringo pulls military rabbits out of his hat, and somehow the son of a bitch has gotten his hands on a long-range field piece!"

"But, sir, our agents also tell us our friends in los Estados

Unidos managed to sidetrack the big guns meant for the rebels."

Another four-pounder came in, over and wide the other way. Maldonado winced and said wearily, "They have us bracketed with the guns they don't have. That tears it. We have to move back poco tiempo!"

"You are ordering a retreat, sir?"

"I am ordering a strategic withdrawal, goddamn your mother's sour milk! I do not wish for to hear that word again! We'll move back just out of range and dig in. Then we'll wait until the big twelve-pounder I sent for gets here. Then we'll huff and we'll puff, and after we knock down the walls we'll go in with buttstock and bayonet. No quarter. I am a reasonable man, but, by the balls of Santiago, those sons of a one-legged whore have spilled the blood of my muchachos, and those rebel bodies we recovered were out of uniform. The rules of civilized warfare are quite clear on that point. Officers and gentlemen do not take mere guerrillas alive!"

The Colombians moved back, spread out, and dug in, deep, outside of Gaston's range without taking any further casualties. None of Gaston's wild shots landed anywhere near anybody, although the noise helped them move pretty well. Maldonado didn't keep all his people out of range. He was an old pro. So he naturally sent out recon patrols, and, since Captain Gringo was a pro too, the next few days were sort of interesting.

Captain Gringo told his own patrol leaders to be careful, so they were. A good jungle scout was hard to find, by either side. Neither big guns nor automatic fire was much use against small parties moving invisibly through tall timber. So the little fighting that took place when patrols bumped into each other was mostly machete work or shoot and run. Both commanders had issued orders to take prisoners if at all possible, but for God's sake to avoid being taken. So in truth there was little blood spilled as both sides ran like hell on making contact. But each contact was recorded with a penciled X on both sides' situation maps. Thus, within forty-eight hours Maldonado and Captain Gringo had felt each other up enough to have a pretty good grasp on who was where with what.

Captain Gringo told El Criado Publico that the enemy was obviously waiting for heavier artillery and offered to lead a combat patrol out to ambush the battery before it could get within range. El Criado Publico refused, saying he wanted his best men and every machine gun on home plate. He probably read more law books than books on military strategy, and he was a stubborn cuss about everything.

Neither Captain Gringo nor Gaston got laid for the next few nights. Whatever the girls had in mind, the soldiers of fortune had to stand alternate guard-mount day and night. Aside from the rebel privates having a tendency to sleep on picket duty, more than a dozen simply vanished as the siege started getting serious.

The alcalde of the village sent a delegation asking permission to evacuate his people. Captain Gringo thought it was a hell of a good idea. But again El Criado Publico was stubborn. He said they would all stand together through thick and thin, and that any villagers who wished to could take shelter within the walls of the fort itself.

There were no takers. The villagers sent no more delegations and at night there were fewer lights burning in the windows down the slope. The experienced soldiers of fortune didn't point this out to the boss. It was no skin off their noses if some pobrecito decided to take his wife and kids on an overnight camping trip, right?

Thus hopefully there weren't too many women and children killed when Maldonado dropped the other shoe late one afternoon. His first long-range shell landed smack in the middle of the fishing village, sending roof tiles flying like red confetti.

Gaston was on watch atop the walls at the time. So Captain Gringo rolled off his bed fully dressed and ran to join him, shouting for one and all he met along the way to take cover and pass it on. Another shell landed on the waterfront as he joined Gaston. He nodded at the mushroom cloud of mud and cobblestones and said, "They're way over."

Gaston uaid, "Oui, but give them time. Firing from a lower position surrounded by tall trees, they of course can't see what they are doing. But I grasp their intent. It's what I would do in their place. They will fire a few more rounds, then knock off and send patrols in after dark to see where they landed, hein?"

Captain Gringo nodded, but said, "Not if I can help it. We'll put out counterpatrols north and south of the hill and make the pricks work at finding out where their first rounds ranged."

Gaston took out a pad and began making notations as he shook his head and said, "It won't work, Dick. They don't have to fall in a shell hole to learn they are firing over the fort. They simply have to make sure no shells landed on *their* side of the ant pile, or the fort itself. Alas, there will be a full moon tonight, too. So the adorable walls of chalk will be visible at some distance."

"Hmm, that gives me an idea. What are you writing?"

Another shell whistled over them to splash loudly but harmlessly into the lagoon. Gaston said, "Merci. With three impact points to work with, an old hand like myself is in business, hein? Regard how they are drawing the segment of a grand circle for me. As I suspected from the intervals, they have one big gun, and, for openers, they are firing at the same elevation each time.''

Captain Gringo nodded in understanding and said, ''So they're firing from the center of said big circle on the map. Let's get to the map and pinpoint the sons of bitches!''

Gaston said, ''I do not have to look at the map. Knowing the curve of the arc, I can tell you from here they are out of range, even for my très formidable long-ranger. Alas, when one has a rifled tube, one does not have to move in close.''

''I said I understood. How far off are they?''

''About five miles behind their front lines. The très fatigue Maldonado has his infantry dug in just out of my range, too. I do wish black sails would appear out there on the horizon, Dick. Staying here much longer could be hazardous to one's health. Maldonado has us outgeneraled as well as outnumbered. The game is about over, and there is no way we can win. He has all the high cards even if we still have the high ground. Why don't we make a run for the border before he closes his noose even tighter, hein?''

Captain Gringo shook his head and said, ''We're not licked yet. Come on, I want you to pinpoint that gun position on the map for me.''

They went down to the office, and as Gaston plotted the big enemy gun on the map, Captain Gringo explained the situation and what he proposed to do about it to El Criado Publico and his top jurados. The old man didn't argue when Jurado Numero Uno insisted on going along on the combat patrol. But he asked, ''For why do you wish for to spill hot tar down the walls facing the jungle, Caltain Gringo?''

The American said, ''Black paint will do if you've got it.

But I'm sure there's plenty of tar in a fishing village. The walls are white coral masonry. By moonlight, and at a safe distance, big black blotches ought to look like artillery strikes. If their scouts report they were on target with their first ranging fire, they won't change the elevation when they open up with solid drum fire and waste it on the far side of the hill."

"I see! But what about my poor villagers?"

"They can rebuild, when and if they ever come back. You may not have noticed it, but most of them have left already, and I don't think the ones who didn't will stay there much longer."

El Criado Publico gasped and said, "They are deserting their country in time of war? Never! I won't hear of it!"

Captain Gringo didn't argue. He knew the old man spent more time with his nose in a book than in the real world. Now that most of the simple peones were safe, probably behind Maldonado's lines and kissing his Colombian ass a lot, there wasn't much anyone could do about it. The hard-core rebels here in the fort had their own asses to worry about.

Gaston looked up and saying, "Violà. The gun position is here and, as I said, well behind a rather solid line of fox holes, Dick. Our scouts say Maldonado's flanks reach a très fatigue distance north and south. It would take you over twelve hours to pussy your foot around either end, spike the gun or more, and get back safely. Alas, the sun would be up again before you got back, if you left at sundown."

Captain Gringo nodded grimly and said, "I can see that. We could hit and run in less than six, if we simply punched through the infantry lines, going and coming."

Jurado Numero Uno gulped and asked, "Won't that be, ah, rather risky, Captain Gringo?"

The tall American said, ''War is a risky business no matter how you do it, muchacho. You can stay here if you like. I'm taking thirty men and a machine gun. Straight in and straight back. I do,'t like to fuck around.''

It wasn't quite that simple. For one thing, the sun refused to go down before at least 6:00 P.M., Panama time. So even after he'd picked and briefed his combat patrol Captain Gringo had some time to kill.

The redhead was nursing her Jim's illness, case of nerves, or whatever the hell was wrong with him. So Captain Gringo gave Gaston a hand as the Frenchman worked on the landward defenses. They both agreed that the Colombian reaction, should the gun-spiking mission succeed, could be an all-out temper tantrum up the slopes from any of three directions.

Gaston left the now-deserted fishing village covered with a four-pounder, just in case, but moved most of the shells and extra machine guns into position to protect the fort from north, west, and south. He ordered his men to sandbag each heavy-weapon's position. The riflemen atop the walls would just have to take their chances. It was more important that they'd be free to shift them a lot as the expected counterattack took a definite shape.

A work detail came back up from the village with buckets of antifouling paint they'd found in the local chandler's abandoned shop. It was park-bench green rather than black, but easier to work with than tar, and it would look just as black by moonlight. The two soldiers of fortune picked spots along the walls to look shell-pocked, but told the camouflage crew just to put the buckets down there for now, of course.

The sun was still hanging around up there when Gaston ran out of things to do. The two soldiers of fortune toured the walls together, looking for possible mistakes or improvements. They couldn't find any. Most of the rebel army would be dug in here with Gaston and the others, whether Captain Gringo and his gang made it back or not. The Frenchman opined that the defenses were a lot stronger than they'd been the time he and a handful of shot-up Legionaires held off the Mexican army of Juarez at Camerone for a few days. On the other hand, the Colombian army was hardly the Mexican army of a generation ago. Maldonado's men were armed with repeating rifles and backed with modern heavy weaponry.

The slopes all around were bare, and thanks to the modest farming of the local villagers there was open flat ground as well for almost half a mile to the nearest tree line. Gaston had considered sending out work crews to move the tree line back a bit. But, as Captain Gringo agreed, they wouldn't be able to push the jungle back enough to matter, and the machete crews would be vulnerable to snipers on the other side.

They ate early with the enlisted men and at last the sun made up its mind to squat among the trees to the west. So Captain Gringo called his men together on the parade and gave them a last pep talk as he waited for it to get really dark. He didn't see Jurado Numero Uno among their nervously smiling faces. He didn't care. But just as it began to look like he was going to get all the credit again, the younger Jurado Numero Ocho puppy-dogged up to him and said he was coming along instead. Numero Uno had to stay and read maps or something with El Criado Publico..

That didn't surprise Captain Gringo. He didn't really want to go himself. He said, "Okay. I've already told these guys the plan, twice. So just stick with me and I'll fill you in as we go. Ah, do you really want to carry that dress saber on a combat patrol?''

The jurado said he did. So Captain Gringo didn't argue. It was now too dark for anyone to tell at a distance whether the gate was open. So he told a couple of proven scouts to take the point, and off they went, with no bands playing and not even one of the two girls they were leaving behind waving them off.

They moved down the slope double-time and then, as planned, spread out and took cover in a corn milpa to see if anybody wanted to argue about it. Captain Gringo had removed the water jacket from one Maxim and was packing it himself. He'd distributed extra machine-gun belts among the men he'd ordered to stick close in case he needed them.

Numero Ocho was sticking even closer. So as they hunkered amid the corn stalks, Captain Gringo gave him a thumbnail briefing, and then, since they couldn't do anything important before his scouts secured their advance to the tree line, he asked the junior officer, ''All bullshit aside, do you have any military training at all?''

Numero Ocho said, ''Not as much as yourself, perhaps, but we are a militant order.''

Captain Gringo frowned and asked, ''Militant order of what? Are you saying the professor recruited you jurados from a fucking *monastery?''*

Numero Ocho shook his head and replied, ''Hardly. We're a celibate as well as a penitent order. The Spanish authorities robbed us of our abbey long ago. Los jurados aave been, how you say, underground since the days of the Inquisition.''

''How come? Weren't even *monks* good enough Catholics for His Most Catholic Majesty?''

''*We* are the true defenders of the faith!'' Numero Uno protested, with a wild gleam in his eye as he added, ''The

Pope at the time was of course corrupt. But no matter. We excommunicated those soft fools in Rome long ago."

Captain Gringo smiled crookedly and asked, "Can you do that? I thought your Pope was supposed to be in charge. Seems to me a Catholic order that fired the Pope would automatically be, well, Protestant."

"Don't be ridiculous! How could we be Protestant? We are, I assure you, more Catholic than any thrice-accursed Italian Pope!"

Captain Gringo didn't want to argue Religion, even with a guy who wasn't an obvious fanatic. But Numero Ocho was wound up and insisted on explaining, "Los jurados are a bunch of the Spanish Knights of the Temple. You have heard of the Knights Templar?"

"I'm afraid the Crusades were a little before my time. I thought the Templars were suppressed by the Church back around 1400 for, ah, certain irregular views."

"They lied. We were neither devil worshippers nor homosexuals. It was all a plot, by the king of France and a corrupt Pope, for to loot our treasuries."

"Yeah, I read about that. They looted you guys pretty good. How did The Templars get so rich back in the middle ages after taking all those vows of poverty? Is there much money in poverty?"

"Be careful, señor. You are beginning to annoy me."

Captain Gringo didn't want to annoy a guy packing a saber. So he dropped it. A few minutes later one of his scouts came in, hunkered down with a wolfish grin, and said, "We just picked off one of their advance pickets, Captain Gringo. He told us the password is 'gato negro' and the countersign is 'perro blanco.' "

"Bueno. Where's the prisoner?"

"Prisoner, Captain Gringo?"

"Never mind. Silly question. Let's move it out."

They did. They made it to the tree line without incident, and when a couple of Colombians sharing a fox hole between two palms cautiously called out, "Gato negro?" a pair of Captain Gringo's guerrillas simply answered, "Sí, perro blanco," and were able to get at them with their silent machetes before they could give the alarm.

So the next few hours were just hard work. It was black at the pit under the forest canopy, and once inside the enemy lines it was a bitch to keep thirty-odd guys going in the right direction, or even to find the right direction. Captain Gringo had a luminous compass dial and it was easy enough to spot the glows of scattered campfires as they worked in deeper. But to avoid them they had to go around, then figure out another heading on the gun position they were trying to reach. Captain Gringo of course had a penciled map copied from the bigger one at headquarters.

But there were no landmarks in a jungle where one dark tree looked much the same as any other. So he had to navigate by dead reckoning and his watch. When the watch said they'd been floundering around in the dark far too long, he called a halt and called in his scouts. He said, "We've overshot. I don't know where the fuck we are, but the gun position we're looking for can't be this far from the fort We're going to have to spread out and move east again very very carefully. I want each man to stay just in visual contact with the guy on either side, and remember we'll be walking, slow, not running. Anyone who spots anything freezes in place and passes the word along the line. With a whisper, not a coyote yell. Any questions? Bueno. Spread out and let's get this show on the road. We haven't got all night and the sun comes up at six A.M. The son of a bitch!"

They moved cautiously abreast back toward the fort. They moved a hell of a distance and Captain Gringo was beginning to wonder if this had been such a hot idea when the man to his right hissed, "Estrada says he sees a light over to the south, Captain Gringo!"

The tall American told the jurado on his left to pass it on and stay put. Then he moved down the line, packing his Maxim, until he too saw a dim orange glow through the trees.

The scout, Estrada, asked if he should move in on it. Captain Gringo said, "No. I'll take the point. I think this must be it, one way or the other. We've chewed up most of the night. So it had *better* be!"

It was. As Captain Gringo moved in, now holding the machine gun on one hip, training the muzzle ahead of him, he eased between two trees just outside the campfire glow and saw a sight for sore eyes.

The long-range twelve-pounder was set up in the middle of a modest clearing, its tube pointed skyward at a forty-five-degree angle. There was a fifteen-man crew of cannoneers and support personnel camped around it in various stages of carelessness. They hadn't even posted pickets this far behind their own lines. They'd built night fires on either side of the big gun and were either bedded down for the night in sleeping bags or sitting up telling dirty stories. They'd pitched no tents. So that big canvas-covered mound across the clearing could only be one thing. He ducked back around the biggest tree bole and hissed to Pablo. When the guerrilla squad leader joined him, he said, "Their ammo is all piled in one place. Far side. Got your dynamite capped?"

"Sí, Captain Gringo. Just point me at their ammo dump and I shall light the fuse."

"I wish you wouldn't, just yet. That comes *after.*"

He started to call in the other leaders. Then he shrugged, figured they'd know what to do, and checked the action of his machine gun before he simply swung back around the tree and moved in, firing from the hip.

The gun crew never had a chance. Most of them died in their sleeping bags before they ever knew what hit them. Those few who leaped to their feet as Captain Gringo traversed the clearing with automatic fire didn't stay there long. He fed them a full belt of hot lead, and then, as his Maxim fell silent to leave everyone still alive with ringing ears, a guerrilla ran up to him with a fresh belt. He put it in, but he didn't need it right now. Nobody on the other side heard ringing or anything else in their ears now.

With the long belt trailing in the dust behind him, Captain Gringo moved across the clearing, stepping over corpses, until he got to the big gun. He leaned the smaller machine gun on the bigger one's trail and opened the breech. Then he took the dynamite charge from his hip pocket and placed it where it would do the most damage to the mechanism. There was a twelve-pounder round in the chamber as well. Pretty sloppy. But it would do even more damage when the dynamite detonated. The gun was of course aimed at the distant fort or rather at the fishing village. So he gave the traverse crank a couple of turns to make sure the only future damage would be one-sided. Then he called out, ''Pablo? You all set?'' And when the guerrilla charging the ammo dump called back he was, the tall American shouted, ''Okay. Vamanos, muchachos, we're lighting the fuses!''

Then he did so, picked up his machine gun, and chased his men into the woods on the far side of the clearing. He ran a football touchdown into the trees before he shouted, ''far 'nough, everybody hit the dirt!'' and suited actions to his words by flopping to the damp forest duff with the Maxim.

Nothing happened for a few seconds. It wasn't supposed to, if he and Pablo had timed things right. Then the charge he'd placed to spike the big gun went off. Loud. He could tell by the whistle from the sky above that the detonation had lobbed the shell as well as gutted the big gun.

It wasn't over. But Jurado Numero-Ocho got to his feet to shout congratulations. Captain Gringo yelled, ''*Down*, dammit!'' and then the ammo dump exploded with a horrendous roar!

The earth heaved like quivering jelly under Captain Gringo's prone form. His ears were jabbed with red-hot ice picks, and somewhere in the jungle a tree fell down with a long scream of protest. Then it got very quiet.

Captain Gringo left the machine gun on the ground as he got to his feet. He saw by the dim light from the distant campfires that others were doing the same. One man leaned against a tree and vomited. But he was in better shape than Jurado Numero Ocho.

Captain Gringo moved closer for a better look. He was sorry he had when he rolled over the blue-clad militant monk. Numero Ocho wasn't a pretty boy anymore. He'd traded in his face for a plate of strawberry jam.

The scout, Estrada, came over to ask if he was dead. Captain Gringo never answered stupid questions if he could help it. He asked Estrada if anyone else had been dumb enough to stand up too soon. When the scout said everyone else was present and accounted for, Captain Gringo said, ''Bueno. We'd better get the hell out of here.''

He started to rise. Then he unbuckled the dead man's belt and pulled Numero Ocho's pants down. Behind him, Estrada whistled and said, "My God, his balls were blown off too? But how? I see no blood down there."

Captain Gringo said, "It was done to him a while back. Okay. Let's move it out."

A few miles away, Colonel Maldonado was mad enough to cut someone's balls off, too.

First he'd been awakened from a pleasant enough dream by the distant thunder of the exploding ammo dump. Then, just as he'd gotten his boots on, an aide came into his command tent to report that some son of a bitch had lobbed a twelve-pound shell into a howitzer position down the line and blown its crew to bloody hash. The four-pounder would probably be all right, once they got it back on its wheels, and by sheer good fortune the enemy shell had missed the howitzer's ammo pile.

Maldonado rubbed a hand over his sleep-numbed face to try to clear his head as he grumbled, "They hit some damned thing with that other round. Tell me about it."

The aide said, "I fear it was our big twelve-pounder, sir. They don't answer on the field wire. Shall I send someone to investigate?"

"Why, no, I thought I'd just consult my crystal ball. Of course I want you to send a runner. You should have done so before now, you stupid offspring of a deaf, dumb, and blind burro! You'd better send an armed patrol in case . . . No, just send a runner. A fast one. You're sure it was a shell, not a spiking patrol, that hit that howitzer crew?"

"Sí, my colonel. From the crater, a twelve-pounder, as I said."

The Colombian commander rubbed his face again, muttering,

"Oh, shit. I was hoping we might trap that crazy Captain Gringo inside our lines. Where in the name of God do you suppose they could have gotten their unwashed hands on a twelve-pounder? Never mind. Get someone over to our own poor twelve-pounder to see if we still have it!"

The aide left. Colonel Maldonado got up and went outside to find his camp in a state of considerable confusion. He was confused too. But he shouted, "At ease, goddamm it! Vegas, front and center!"

His adjutant ran up to him and saluted. Maldonado returned the salute wearily and said, "We're in trouble, Vegas. The rains are coming on. We're outgunned. This isn't going to work."

"Are we to retreat then, my colonel?"

"Don't talk dirty. *Retreat* is a word that is not in my vocabulary. On the other hand, there's no sense in banging one's head against a stone wall. Perhaps, after the rains, with more men and material . . ."

A scout came running up to them, saluted, and said breathlessly, "We have just viewed the old Spanish fortress, my colonel."

"And?"

"And there are three very big gaps blown in the landward walls. The light was not good. But the coral blocks glow pale in the moonlight and . . ."

Maldonado silenced him with a wave and said, "Bueno. Our big gun was right on target with its first ranging rounds after all! It's about time *we* had some luck around here!"

He turned to his adjutant and said, "We attack at once. Move the howitzers into range and tell them I want a heavy screening barrage. They are to cease fire at 0500 so our infantry can move up the slopes in the last hour of darkness. What are you waiting for? Are you deaf?"

The adjutant said, "But, sir, you were just about to order a re . . . ah, strategic withdrawal, no?"

"Are you mad as well as deaf? We've breached their walls in at least three places! We'd never be able to explain pulling back now. Not without at least one all-out effort. So let's*do* it, muchacho. Buttstock and bayonet, with shirkers to be shot on the spot by their squad leaders. Oh, yes, tell the buglers to sound 'no quarter' when they blow the charge. I've had just about enough of this shit."

When the barrage began a little after 0430, Gaston did what he could to discourage it with counterbattery fire, and since Gaston was a hell of an artilleryman, with his own guns well sandbagged and firing from higher ground, he did pretty well. The Colombians had more howitzers to begin with, but as the sly old Frenchman layed his own guns to answer the muzzle flashes he could see so well from the top of the hill, the Columbians began to loose gun crews and, with one lucky rebel round, another whole ammo dump.

But war is a cruel mistress, and it cost the fort a lot of window glass, some masonry, and one of Gaston's gun crews before the enemy ceased fire.

El Criado Publico, his senior staff officers, and other noncombatants had of course taken cover within the thick inner walls. But some of the junior jurados were trying to be useful. So when one asked Gaston what the sudden silence meant, the little Frenchman growled, "Infantry for breakfast. Keep your head down. They'll be shooting as they come up the slope any moment now."

A regular guerrilla noncom joined them to report that all the machine-gun crews were set. Gaston told him to keep his head down, too. Gaston was in a foul mood this morning, and the attack he was braced for was only part of it. He didn't like the people up here very much, and his young friend, Captain Gringo, was still out there somewhere behind the enemy lines, if he was still alive. Gaston could only hope he hadn't been killed by friendly fire as he'd lobbed four-pounders freely into the dark jungle.

A tinny bugle blew somewhere in the darkness. Gaston nodded grimly and said, "Shame on you, Maldonado. Even the Mexicans under Juarez took prisoners. But then, Juarez was a gentleman, non?"

The eastern sky was just beginning to pearl gray when the Colombian skirmish line started up the slope from the west. Gaston couldn't depress his four-inchers to blast them. So now it was up to the machine gunners and riflemen along the walls on either side of them. Gaston waited until he could have seen the whites of their eyes, had it been lighter out, then drew his .38, chose a noncom in the lead for his target, and signaled "open fire" as he blew the Colombian back down the slope.

The others around him shot pretty good too. So the first skirmish line was shot down in a dead and dying windrow as yet another line came out of the tree line at the fort.

It was sheer slaughter. By not all one-sided. The Colombian regulars fired back with repeating rifles as they charged. So by sheer luck they had to hit somebody atop the walls from time to time, and did. A bullet spanged close to Gaston, showering him with powerdered coral as, at his feet, a guerrilla writhed, gun-shot, sobbing for his mother. Gaston shot him in the head to put him out of his misery, then went back to peppering the men coming up the slope at him.

A scalding party ran for one of the painted "gaps" with a ladder. They got close enough to fall down looking surprised as hell as a machine gun swept across them. Gaston sighed and said, "So much for camouflage. I was wondering why they were behaving so strangely this morning!"

Maldonado's men wouldn't have gotten through in any case, most likely. But to add to their dismay, as the third suicide line left the tree line, Captain Gringo stepped out of the same trees, flanking them, and raked them with a long burst of machine-gun fire while his guerrillas used their rifles to pop off the few not in his line of fire.

Up the line, Colonel Maldonado, like most commanders in the middle of a battle, only had a hazy grasp of the overall picture. But he could see, as he swept the slope with field glasses, that his plan obviously needed more work. He'd already expended more casualties than he really felt like explaining to his superiors, and so far nobody had gotten anywhere near even one of those gaps in the walls up above.

As the light got better, Maldonado adjusted the focus of his powerful field glasses, had another look at a "gap," and roared like a bull with a broomstick up its ass.

"Oh, the treacherous murdering son of a defrocked Jesuit and a whoring nun!" he shouted to everyone in range.

An aide ran up to him, sobbing, "We are flanked, my colonel! They are chopping us up with machine-gun fire from the south!"

"That's what I just said!" yelled Maldonado, shaking a futile fist at the walls up the slope as he protested, "That was a rotten trick, even for a gringo!"

His aide looked bewildered. Maldonado was feeling the same. But he had sense enough to call out, "Sound the . . . withdrawal. They painted those apparent breaches as a ruse, and now, goddamn their black gringo hearts, they have us in a death trap! Vamanos, compañeros! This is no place for a civilized soldado this morning!''

So the Colombian column retreated, whether they called it that or not. Captain Gringo didn't risk moving out into the open before his own scouts reported that the Colombians were pulling out for sure. Then he still waited. The day dawned gray and overcast, with the smell of rain on its breath. Captain Gringo waited until the Colombian troops were marching south through a light drizzle before he led his own party up to the fort for congratulations.

Everyone seemed happy as hell, save for Gaston. Captain Gringo noted the expression on his old friend's face, but didn't comment on it until they could speak privately. That took some time. El Criado Publico was as enthusiastic as a little kid about what he called his victory, and wanted Captain Gringo to go right back out and round up the villagers hiding in the jungle. One could get the impression he was anxious to get back to running his utopia right away.

Captain Gringo talked him out of it by pointing out that the lost sheep would probably come home wagging their tails behind them once they, too, made sure the Colombians had called the game because of rain and other discomforts. He said, ''Maldonado just left a lot of unburied dead. I guess that's allowed down here. But let's keep an eye peeled anyway. They may try to recover at least the officers, come dark.''

El Criado Publico nodded grimly and said, ''Not if we get to them first. I intend to burn them all, as an example.''

Captain Gringo frowned and asked, ''Example to who? That's not the way it's done, boss. They'll keep the way they are, for now. Then, with your permission, I'll see they're buried with full military honors."

"Permission denied! Why would we wish for to honor enemy dead, young man?"

"Oh, I dunno. Maybe because they were soldiers who died bravely, enemy or not. Let's not argue about it. If you want to burn them, bury them, or stuff them, it's not gonna bother them much, so I'm not gonna let it bother me. If you'll excuse me, I'd like to take a bath and put on something dry. You want to scrub my back, Gaston?"

The Frenchman said he did, and so, there being no objections, the two soldiers of fortune left the office. As soon as they were alone, Captain Gringo said, "You did pretty good up here. What's eating you?"

Gaston said, "I would have been long gone, had not you been out in the jungle fighting for these lunatics. Last night, right after you left, I helped Inocencia look for her pussy."

"You hadn't already found it? Oh, you mean the pet jaguar she's so fond of."

"Oui. We were unable to get to it. The girl is in her room at the moment, pouting about it. But she did show me something I want you to see. You'd never believe me if I simply told you."

Gaston looked around, made sure there was nobody else in the corridor with them, and led Captain Gringo to a nondescript door. He opened it on utter darkness, pulled the younger man inside, and shut it before he said, "We are in some sort of ventilation shaft, built by the old Spanish engineers. In fairness to them, I think the pits of justice were originally intended as powder magazines. Watch your adorable head until your eyes get used to the light. Inocencia told me she discovered this unused passage by accident as she wandered about in her boredom. The regular passage leading to the dungeons on a lower level is guarded day and night. She hoped we would be able to get as far as the cell they have her pet locked up in. We could not. But we saw what I am about to show you. Even Inocencia was shocked, and if half the things she told me are at all true, she should not shock easily, hein?''

As Captain Gringo grew accustomed to the dark he saw faint patches of light strung out ahead. He said, ''Lead on. I'd like to see what could shock a girl who sucks off cats and says she lost her baby cherry to her own father!''

Gaston said, ''Keep your voice down. Those are ventilating grilles in the ceilings of the cells below. Hopefully neither the prisoners nor guards have any interest in where the stink might rise to, hein?''

''Jesus, it sure does smell bad in here. That's not a big cat. It smells like a *corpse!*''

Gaston nodded and led him to the first grille. As they hunkered down they could see down into the cell below. A naked man was strapped in a solid oak chair, bolted to the floor. A rubber tube was shoved up one nostril, taped to his forehead and leading to a funnel attached to the back of the chair behind his head. Gaston whispered, ''The girl explained the way they force feed him. Apparently she'd seen that before. The tube leads down to his stomach. Once a day they pour him full of banana pulp and canned milk. They can keep him alive a long time that way. But, as you see, and no doubt smell, he is forced to sit there in his own filth.''

''It sure looks like a boring way to serve a sentence. Know what he's in for?''

''Oui; Inocencia explained he was the village photographer. When he was not photographing weddings and funerals, he liked to take dirty pictures. When los jurados raided his studio, they found photographs of little white girls and full-grown; well-developed African gentlemen. The usual muck one buys on any street corner in Paris or New York. You can't see them from up here, but the cell walls are papered with filthy photographs. Some new and no-doubt inspiring to our friend below. Inocencia says she was asked to pose for some rather shocking photos by her stern but just father."

Captain Gringo frowned and whispered, "Gaston, that's just plain nuts! How can El Criado punish a pornographer if he takes dirty pictures of his own daughter?"

"I too found that très confusing. Inocencia explained that her father considers himself above the law he judges others so severely by. At any rate, he got her to do it. It is not as if they are strangers. She assured me it was all quite correct. There was nobody else in the room and he remained fully dressed as he got her to bend over and, ah, open her lips."

Captain Gringo gagged and said, "Okay. I'm shocked. By the way, did you know los jurados are some kind of castrated penitent order of defrocked monks?"

Gaston sighed and said, "It doesn't surprise me. As one dirty old man to another, I was wondering how El Criado managed to keep his pants on while he was posing his très belle daughter in such interesting positions. She says he stopped screwing her every night right after he took up with these weird younger fanatics. Do you suppose . . . ?"

"Could be. They all sound pretty weird. When does that poor guy down there get out?"

"Never, according to Inocencia. He simply gets to sit there looking at dirty pictures until he dies, no doubt très sick of his hobby."

"I can see he doesn't have a hard-on right now. But, Jesus, if they keep force feeding him, he could last indefinitely!"

"Oui. Let me show you more draconian justice, Dick."

They moved to another vent. Below, another naked form was strapped the same way in a similar chair. But this prisoner was a woman of about fifty, with a gag in her mouth as well as a tube up her nose as she stared, wild-eyed, at nothing at all. She wasn't attractive and, like the other prisoner, sat in a brown pile of her own inevitable body processes. She looked about eight-months' pregnant. Gaston said she wasn't, explaining, "Her crime was usury. She was the village money lender, and she charged more interest than one is allowed to, in utopia. So every day they come in and force more money down her throat. Some of the silver dollars donated by El Criado's American backers, no doubt. She could shit nickels and dimes. But, as you see, she is accumulating interest indeed as the silver just remains in her stomach. I don't see how she can last much longer, even though one's belly can distend amazingly, a meal of silver at a time, hein?"

"Oh, Jesus, that's just *sick,* Gaston!"

"Oui. But as we go on it gets sicker. Hold your nose before you look down into the next cell."

Captain Gringo didn't. He just breathed shallowly as they peeked down through the next vent. He was used to the smell of death. Though there sure was a lot of it in the air right now.

The punishment below had been varied to the extent that the prisoner was spread-eagled flat on the floor, albeit with the same tube up his nose to keep him alive, and probably naked. It was hard to tell. A woman lay atop him, her bloated purple buttocks covering the prisoner's lap. She too was held atop him in a spread-eagle position, with wrists and ankles shackled to rings set in the stone floor. The man's eyes were open and staring up at the grille, but blind with madness, and the two soldiers of fortune were invisible to him in the darkness in any case.

Gaston said, "This one was a rapist murderer. The other villagers reported him to El Criado Publico for judgment. As you see, our host judges harshly."

"Kee-rist! Is that his *victim* they have rotting on top of him?"

"Mais non, that would hardly be just, according to our enlightened despot, Zagal. The village woman he strangled and raped was of course given a Christian burial, as an obviously innocent victim. The beauty of the punishment below, as Inocencia explained it, is that a man who enjoys rutting with dead women should be allowed to do so forever. She's been embalmed, albeit not too skillfully, as one can sniff, and her vagina is filled with petroleum jelly, lest it dry out and spoil the pleasure, hein?"

"Good God! You mean that poor bastard's cock is actually in that overripe corpse down there? Come on, who could keep it up under such conditions?"

Gaston said, "He has little choice. They have been sewn together with butcher's twine. No doubt it must be soft, most of the time, but the devilish ingenuity of the punishment is that human nature being what is is, he can't remain uninspired *all* the time, with his shaft inside a well-greased and très tight pussy. It is tight, of course, thanks to more butcher's twine. The last time I looked, he was pumping up into her hot and heavy, meanwhile crying hysterically. At the moment he would seem to be between orgasms, non?"

Captain Gringo swallowed the green taste in his mouth and muttered, "Okay. The guy's a murderer and a rapist, but enough's enough!"

Gaston shook his head and said, "They have assured him

that when one falls apart they mean to provide him with another dead lover. He comes from a big family."

"A big *what*? That's one of his *relatives* they've sewn his dong into?"

"Oui, it's his mother. One imagines that might add to the horror of his position, non? Think what it would feel like to be forced to stare into one's own mother's face as she decomposes with your cock in her."

"I'd rather not. But if that's *justice*, I'm as nuts as Zagal! How could even a madman justify the death of that poor slob's mother? *She* didn't rape anybody, did she?"

"Mais non, but she did raise a rapist murderer to manhood, non? As Inocencia explains it, they were kind enough to strangle her in front of her son before they forced him to fornicate with her corpse. As he does so, at least three or four times a day no matter how he tries not to, he must be cheered immensely by the thought that once she gets too rotten they intend to replace her with his sister's *fresher* corpse. Inocencia says they started with the older, less attractive woman so he could have something to look forward to with mixed emotions. I understand the sister who comes next is young and beautiful. The guards will no doubt be amused by his reluctant lust, hein?"

Captain Gringo swore and reached in his jacket for his .38. Gaston grabbed his arm and hissed, "Mais non! Don't you think *I* carry a gun anymore? That poor bastard is done for in any case. I, for one, am not at all interested in learning what sort of justice El Criado Publico would find apt for idealists who did not admire his idealism!"

Captain Gringo grimaced and said, "When you're right you're right. The guy's probably totally insane by now anyway."

"Oui; he's starting to fuck his dead mother again. There is

only one more cell we can get above via this old tunnel. Do you want to see what they do to common thieves, Dick?"

"No, thanks, I've seen enough to convince me these guys are sadistic lumatics. Let's get out of here. If I'd known then what I know now, I sure could have saved lots of running around last night. Los jurados make a mere pisspot dictatorship look like kid stuff!"

"Oui. I too was forced to fight for the wrong side last night, as I waited for my wayward child to come home. Now that I have you back in my arms, do you agree we ought to drag ass tout de suite?"

Captain Gringo waited until they were back outside and safe for the moment before he said, "We can't cut out just yet. We have to wait for Esperanza, and Bowman and the redhead are innocent bystanders, too!"

Gaston wrinkled his nose and said, "Mais non, the redhead is a stupid little slut, Bowman is a species of idiot, and Esperanza is in no danger from los jurados. They need her services; besides, she and her tough crew can look after themselves should los jurados go crazy. hein?"

"What do you mean, *should* they go crazy? They're already crazy as bedbugs, and it gets worse. With the Colombian army pulling out, the villagers will be coming back!"

"Maybe they won't. They must know a little of what has been going on up here, from the frightened way they've been acting, non?"

Captain Gringo shook his head wearily and said, "They're poor simple losers, Gaston. They'll come back for the same reason peasants in other parts go on living in a flood plain or on the slopes of an active volcano. They just don't have anyplace else to go."

Gaston said. "They really should consider moving, this time. But you are probably right. Eh bien, what can we do about it, now that we have managed to save the dictatorship of El Criado Publico?''

Captain Gringo said flatly, ''That's easy. We're going to have to overthrow it, of course!''

They couldn't just start wrecking the joint. For one thing, the odds were lousy, and, for another, at least half the people around them might not deserve to be wrecked. The two soldiers of fortune had been recruited to serve as officers, and it had still taken them this long to discover they were working for one or more homicidal lunatics.

Captain Gringo agreed that most of the enlisted men serving under him and Gaston would probably be shocked to learn about the grim sights they'd just seen, but warned, ''We're going to have to be careful as hell trying to separate the sheep from the goats, Gaston. Guess wrong on one teacher's snitch and . . . I wonder what El Criado Publico would consider the proper punishment for plotting a counter-revolution.''

''Sacreblue! Let us hope we never find out! As the plot thickens, I can see it may call for some trés careful stirring indeed, non?''

''Yeah, we'd better just lay low like the tar baby until we figure out just what the fuck we're plotting!''

So they didn't tell anybody that El Criado Publico was nuts, for the time being. By later in the day the rain was coming down fire and salt and the villagers started coming in from the jungle, saving the rebel army some patrolling when they reported that the Colombian column had indeed gone for good, leaving considerable spoils behind.

When Gaston suggested sending out a detail to salvage the

abandoned ordnance and any ammo the regulars might have left, El Criado Publico said not to bother, as he had all the guns he needed to hold the fort against all comers. Neither soldier of fortune argued. They knew Maldonado would be back as soon as the rain let up, but with luck they wouldn't be here. So what the hell.

Captain Gringo did argue, gently, when El Criado Publico ordered the alcalde of the village executed for desertion in the face of the enemy. But before the argument could get serious, it developed that the alcalde had solved the problem by leaving with the Colombian army, along with half-a-dozen other village leaders who had decided on the devil they knew.

The old man agreed, grudgingly, that it made little sense to execute the dimwits who'd come back to him, although he called them patriotic subjects rather than dimwits. He settled for having the villagers get rid of the bodies scattered over the slopes to the west. He'd apparently given up the idea of cremating them in a tropic rainstorm. So in the end they at least got buried, albeit with neither military honors nor the rites of their faith. The village priest had been pretty smart, too. He'd probably be back when he read in the Panama City papers that the area was once more under Colombian control.

Late that afternoon, the redheaded Martha asked Captain Gringo to come with her. But when she led him into Jim Bowman's room, he saw that she hadn't meant it the way he'd hoped. Bowman was sick as a dog. Captain Gringo sat on the edge of the bed, felt his forehead, pried up an eyelid, and said, "Welcome to the club, Bowman. You've got yellow jack."

The redhead gasped and said, "Oh, no! Is he going to die? Is it catching?"

Captain Gringo said, "It looks like a real dose, and nobody knows for sure how you catch it. There's a Spanish doctor who keeps saying yellow jack's spread by mosquitoes. Everybody else keeps telling him he's crazy."

"Oh, God, I've been bit by oodles and oodles of mosquitoes since we got here!" she sobbed, adding, "I want to go home. I don't want to die of yellow jack!"

He said, "Take it easy. Obviously every mosquito can't carry yellow jack or everyone would catch it down here. That's one of the holes in that Spanish doctor's theory." He saw some brown pills on the bed table near the feverish man's head and added, "Don't give him any more quinine. It doesn't help yellow jack and it'll only upset his stomach worse."

He asked the sick fellow American if he'd puked black bile yet, and when Bowman said he'd puked a bucketful that morning, but nothing black, Captain Gringo told the redhead to keep him drinking plenty of liquids whether he wanted to or not. She looked like she was ready to throw up too. So he said, "Look, I'll see about getting him an orderly. It's almost dinnertime. Why don't you go freshen up? I'll handle this."

She said, "I'm scared! I want to go home!"

He nodded and said, "No problem. Esperanza should be here with her schooner anytime now. I'll see you're both put aboard and she'll run you back to civilization, okay?"

Bowman stared up owlishly and said, "We can't leave now! I have to help old Zagal set up his democracy, American-style! Can't have these greasers screwing up, now that we've helped them win."

Captain Gringo looked disgusted and said, "Nobody's won anything down here, you poor simp! The Colombians have conceded a round because they don't like standing in the rain. The so-called democracy you and the people you work for are backing is never going to get anywhere. Los jurados don't know what a democracy is, and old Zagal belongs on a funny farm! When the *Nombre Nada* arrives, I'm putting you two lost lambs aboard her, period. I frankly don't give a damn about your health, Bowman. But Red, here, is a good kid, and it's gonna get rough as hell around here poco tiempo!''

Bowman started making a patriotic speech in bed. Captain Gringo rose and led the redhead out, saying he'd meet her later when dinner was served. Then he ducked in long enough to tell Bowman to shut up and that he'd be right back. He went and found a servant to deal with the sick man. Then he went to his room to wash up for dinner. As long as he was there, he took a peek through the pinhole. But Inocencia wasn't there, with or without Gaston.

Gaston met him in the hall instead. The Frenchman said, ''I just saw a beautiful sight from the walls above. La *Nombre Nada* has arrived. May I make a mild suggestion, Dick?''

Captain Gringo said, ''I'm way ahead of you. I've been thinking it over and there's no way we're going to put these maniacs out of business without a lot of innocent bystanders getting hurt as well. Bowman's down with yellow jack. I just told him and the redhead we're putting them aboard Esperanza's shooner. I think we'd better leave with them. Colombia isn't paying us. Let *them* do something about this stupid situation!''

Gaston grinned and said, ''I would kiss you, if I was not worried about my reputation! That's the sweetest thing you've said to me all day! Shall I scamper down to tell Esperanza our plans? By the way, since you can't possibly use both women once aboard la *Nombre Nada* . . .''

''We'll work that out later,'' Captain Gringo cut in, adding, ''Right now we'd better go to dinner and act innocent. Esperanza won't unload for a while and we'll sort of stroll down casually, once our host is relaxed, see?''

It didn't work. El Criado Publico *looked* relaxed, and seemed polite as ever, when the two soldiers of fortune joined him and his other guests at the table. Inocencia wasn't there yet. The redhead was. Seated next to her, in the missing Bowman's place, was Esperanza. All things considered, she didn't seem as happy to see him as one might have expected. In fact she looked upset as hell about something.

Captain Gringo smiled pleasantly across at his old gal pal as he took his own seat. He wondered if the big Basque brunette and the sassy smaller redhead had been comparing notes about him. It hardly seemed they'd had time. He said, "I thought you usually stayed on board, Esperanza."

She shot a wary glance at the old man seated at the head of the table and said, "So did I. I have never been marched to dinner at gunpoint before."

Captain Gringo didn't know how to answer that as Gaston, at his side, murmured, "Oh, merde!" So he didn't try.

El Criado Publico smiled pleasantly and explained, "I wanted you all here this evening for to help me celebrate my great victory over the forces of evil. Where is Jurado Numero Segundo? I do not see my daughter, either. Oh, well, no matter. All the people I find *amusing* are here. Shall we have the soup before I tell you about the traitors in our midst?"

Captain Gringo frowned and asked him what the hell he was talking about. The rebel leader shrugged and said, "Before we dine? Very well, since you are one of the traitors under discussion. You see, I learned just this evening that you are planning to desert me. Is that the way you repay my many kindnesses, Captain Gringo?"

The tall American shot a hard look at the redhead across from him. She shook her head and said, "Honest, it wasn't me, Dick!"

El Criado Publico purred, "La señorita speaks the truth. I see she has chosen her side unwisely, as well. If you must know, Señor Bowman was good enough to confide in the servant you were kind enough to fetch for him just a little while ago."

Captain Gringo pasted a smile across his suddenly numb lips and said, "For Pete's sake, boss, a man's delirious with fever! I don't know what he told your spy, but if you think someone's plotting against you . . ."

"I do not think," El Criado Publico cut in, smiling at the redhead as he added, "La Señorita Pendergast was here before you two traitors arrived, and, as you may have noticed, she is not intelligent enough to keep a secret. I was able to verify, with innocent questions, what you told her and Bowman, eh?"

The redhead pouted and said, "That's not fair! When you said you wished us a pleasant voyage, how was I to know you were an old sneak?"

Zagal said, "I am perhaps, as you say, and old sneak, señorita. I am also the dictator of this republic, and a man in my position can afford to take no chances."

Esperanza yawned elaborately and asked, "What has all this cat-and-mouse business to do with me and my crew, El Criado? Nobody told *me* anything about anything."

"True, my gunrunning beauty. On the other hand, with you here as my guest, your vessel would hardly put out to sea before I wanted it to, eh?"

"Oh, for God's sake. Don't you want me to go back to Limón for more guns and ammunition?"

"All in good time, señorita. The tide shall not turn before midnight. I may send Bowman, at least, back with you. I am still trying to make up my mind what to do about these other guests. Does anyone here have any suggestions? What about you, Numero Uno?"

The senior jurado present shrugged and said, "Why not just shoot the three of them, sir?"

Captain Gringo braced himself to rise and draw at the same time. But then something that certainly felt like a pistol barrel nudged the base of his skull from behind, so he froze, as hands from off stage disarmed him and Gaston at the same time.

El Crriado Publico chuckled and said, "That's better. I think it might be fitting to allow Captain Gringo to die as he has lived, by the machine gun. Gaston, on the other hand, might prefer being tied to the muzzle of a cannon. A fitting death for an old artilleryman, no? I am not yet sure what we do with beautiful but dumb redheads."

Martha began to cry. Esperanza put an arm around her shoulders and said, "Hush. Can't you take a joke?"

"I don't think he's kidding!" wailed the redhead.

They never found out. At that moment the regal Inocencia walked in, flanked by her black jaguar on one side and the jurado called Numero Segundo on the other. They were followed by a squad of other, lesser jurados. El Criado Publico frowned the length of the table at his daughter and asked, "How did you get that damned beast back? I gave orders it was to remain locked up until the emergency was over!"

Inocencia smiled back coldly and said, "Diablo and me could not wait until your emergency was over, father. There is always an emergency when *you* are around! I am sorry, but you have become senile as well as crazy. So it is time for to end it."

The old man leaped to his feet, sending his chair crashing backward as he gasped. "You speak to me that way? You dare? Numero Segundo, you are closer to my wicked child. Sieze her!"

The jurado drew his revolver instead, saying, "I am Numero *Uno* now, por favor."

The older jurado nearer the head of the table leaped to his feet, protesting, "But *I* am Numero Uno!"

So the one with the gun said softly, "Not anymore," and blew his face off.

Captain Gringo didn't stay to see the whole show. So he couldn't tell just who was shooting at whom as he kicked himself over backward, chair and all, and hit the floor rolling, as the room filled with noise and gunsmoke. As he tried to get his bearings, somebody put a round in one of the guys who'd disarmed him, and his purloined .38 bounced off the rug between him and the table. He said, "Muchas gracias!" and crawled under the table with it.

He met Esperanza and the redhead there. He said, "Great minds crawl in the same channels. Are you both okay?"

The redhead sobbed as she said, "Someone's lying across my ankles and he's all icky!" So Captain Gringo put down the gun and hauled her all the way under as Esperanza asked what the hell was going on.

He said, "Palace coup, I think. We'd better get out of here before either side wins! Stay put a second."

He stuck his head out the side he'd been seated on, saw nothing much but a blue haze of gunsmoke, and told Esperanza, "There's a window just past the first overturned chair you'll hit. Get Red out while I cover you."

The American girl protested, "I'm scared! I feel safer here!"

Esperanza swore in Basque, grabbed a fistful of Martha's red hair, and started dragging her after her as she growled, "Jesus, you're stupid."

Captain Gringo rose to one knee to make sure nobody tried to stop them. A hazy figure in the swirling smoke spotted him and tried to part his blond hair with a bullet. So Captain Gringo shot the son of a bitch, whoever he was. Somewhere n the confusion, Inocencia was shouting, "Enough! Cease fire! The situation is under my complete control!" So he knew she had to be as crazy as her old man.

He called out, "Gaston?" and was answered by a pistol shot that just missed his ear in the blue haze. So he didn't do that anymore. He saw that the girls had made it out. He took a deep breath, leaped to his feet, and dived headfirst out the open window.

He landed on one shoulder and rolled to his feet as Esperanza shouted, "This way, Dick!"

He saw the two of them moving down the veranda in the dim but thank God smokeless light and chased after them, gun in hand. Ahead, a blue-clad jurado stepped out of a doorway to bar their path. The two girls were in Captain Gringo's line of fire. But Esperanza solved the problem by nailing him with a beautiful left hook, and when he hit the deck and tried to get up, the redhead kicked him in the head, and that was that.

Captain Gringo took the lead, found a stairway leading down, and led them down it. They beelined across the rainswept parade for the gate on the far side. It was dark as hell. But when they made it to the gun position out in the middle of the open expanse, he was able to make out cotton-clad figures coming the other way. So he got the girls behind the howitzer and called out, "Quien es?"

One of the squad leaders who'd been with him in action called back, "Is that you, Captain Gringo? What's going on?"

'Office politics. Which side are you on, Pablo?"

"*Your* side, of course! Your comrade, Lieutenant Verrier, is holding the gate with other sensible people. He sent us to look for you in case you needed help."

"I do. Take these women to him and tell him I'll be along shortly."

He patted Esperanza on her ample rump and added, "Get going, querida! I'll meet you at the schooner, I hope. If I don't make it, thanks for the memories."

The redhead wailed, "What about my Jim?" So Esperanza just grabbed her by the wrist and hauled the dumb little dame in her wake as she tore after the other guerrillas for the gatehouse.

Captain Gringo holstered his revolver, bent down to grab the wet steel trail of the four-pounder, and heaved. It didn't want to move until he put his wet back into it. As he got it off the mud, he swiveled the field piece around to train its muzzle on the headquarters side. As he dropped the trail and opened the breech, a familiar male voice shouted, "Cease fire, damm it! Man the walls, my loyal muchachos! We must not let that schooner get away!"

Captain Gringo muttered, "Shit. I was betting on Inocencia winning," as he picked up a shell, slammed it home, shut the breech, and pulled the lanyard.

The fort had been built to stand up to fire from outside, not inside. So as the howitzer recoiled and slammed a four-pound shell through the thinner stone walls of El Criado Publico's headquarters at point-blank range, and went off inside, the windows lit up like jack o' lantern eyes and glass rained down all around Captain Gringo. But he was on a roll, and figured it couldn't hurt to hit 'em again. So he reloaded and gave them another point-blank cannon shot.

The fort's ammo had been stored for safety in separate magazines under each angle of the fort. So *all* the ammo on hand didn't explode at once when his second shell got lucky. Just enough to knock him on his ass in the rain as the whole interior of the fort was illuminated in brilliant orange and filled with thunderous echoes.

He rolled over and flattened tight against the ground until most of the heavier debris had finally thudded down around him. Then he leaped up and ran for the gate.

Gaston ran out in the rain to meet him, saying, "It's about time you got here, you destructive child. Look what I found for you to play with."

Captain Gringo took the machine gun from Gaston and kept going, the ammo belt lashing behind him like a dragon's tail as he asked, "Did you send the girls on to the boat?"

"Mais non, our passage to the waterfront seems to be disputed. A species of jurado has a squad out in the rain, pegging shots at one and all who try to leave the party. They must have been pulling MP duty in the village and . . ."

"Never mind what they're doing there," Captain Gringo cut in. "We have to make it to the schooner before El Criado gets a handle on the situation!"

"Could the maniac still be alive, Dick? For a machine gunner, you fire a mean cannon!"

By now they were in the gate tunnel, where a hundred or more guerrillas and the two girls seemed to be stuck. Captain Gringo shoved his way through. He noticed Esperanza had picked up a gun in her travels and was at his elbow as he neared the outside exit. He asked her where the hell she thought she was going, and Esperanza said, "With you, to the death!"

He didn't have time to argue. So he just told her she was nuts as he stepped out into the rain again, firing the Maxim from the hip.

There were times for scientific warfare, but this wasn't one of 'em. The loyalist jurados down the slope had the gate zeroed in, and the longer a guy spent pussyfooting out, the better target he made. So Captain Gringo simply gave them a target moving fast and shooting back as he charged down the slope at them, hosing wildly with automatic fire.

Behind him, someone shouted, "Viva Captain Gringo!" and the whole band of confused guys on his side exploded out the gate, shooting confusedly but mostly in the right direction.

Los jurados had the initial advantage of prone positions and rifles trained on a known attack approach. So some of the guerrillas on Captain Gringo's side were hit as he led the charge. But los jurados lost anyway, as they were simply crushed by superior numbers and fire power.

At the bottom of the slope, after running over the dopes who'd tried to prevent him from reaching it, Captain Gringo dropped the hot and empty Maxim in the mud and called a hault to count noses.

Gaston and the two girls were still with him. So were Pablo and most of the others. Captain Gringo said, "We don't have room on the schooner for all you guys, Pablo. On the other hand, there's plenty of abandoned army supplies in the jungle over that way, and the Costa Rican border's not too far. Deal?"

Pablo grinned wolfishly and replied, "Only the first part, amigo mio! I think I just made general. Most of the others hiding in the cellars will no doubt join me, once the dust settles. It is time someone showed Panama a *sensible* revolution! I shall take everyone over to the high country to the west with plenty of arms, food, and of course adelitas, to mount a practical guerrilla action, eh?"

Captain Gringo didn't argue. One more bandit band wasn't going to make much difference down here, and it wasn't his problem. He nodded and said, "Good hunting. Gaston, help Esperanza with that redhead. She looks like she's about to faint."

Gaston said he wanted to carry Martha's more interesting parts. But the redhead said, "I'm all right. I'm just so worried about my Jim. We have to go back for him."

So Gaston picked her up, threw her over his shoulder, and said, "Lead on, Dick," and, as Captain Gringo took Esperanza's hand to do so, the Frenchman patted the redhead's ass and explained, "If he was not blown to bits he was going to die of yellow jack in any case, my pet. But do not worry. I promise you shall not be allowed to feel lonely on the way back to Limón."

As they headed for the waterfront they were met by some of Esperanza's crew, armed and dangerous. They said the way to the coast was clear. The villagers, as usual, wanted no part of the action.

So a few minutes later they were all aboard the *Nombre Nada*, and, low tide or not, Esperanza ordered them to cast off and back off muy pronto. She'd of course kept up her steam all this time, while the cargo of arms they hadn't finished unloading would fetch a nice price somewhere up or down the coast where other rebels might be more reasonbale.

The she-skipper had to stay on deck while all this was going on. Captain Gringo kept her company despite the rain. They were both already soaked to the skin, but that was okay. They still had most of the night ahead of them to undress and get warmed up.

Gaston saw no reason to stay out in the rain. So he carried the redhead to his stateroom and bolted the door before he set her on her feet, saying, "Don't sit on the bed until I get you out of those wet clothes, hein?"

As he began to undress her, the redhead protested, "What are you doing? This is not my cabin and . . . *Sir!* That's not a button you're fumbling with!"

Gaston hauled her in and kissed her to shut her up as he let her wet garments fall to the floor and unbuckled his own belt with his free hand.

Martha responded warmly to his kisses. She didn't know how to kiss any other way. But as Gaston moved her over to the bed and lowered her cool, damp, naked body to it, she gasped and said, "Wait, this is all so sudden! I'm engaged!"

Gaston said, "Not yet," as he forced her clammy thighs apart with his own small but strong legs and got his erection in position. She gasped again in mingled surprise and pleasure as he entered her and said, "*Now* you are engaged, M'mselle, in a très delightful way, non?"

"Oh, dear, I seem to be getting raped," said the redhead, as she raised her knees and locked her ankles across the little Frenchman's bounding buttocks. He soothed, "Mais non, my child, it is only rape when you do not *enjoy* it!"

She giggled and clamped down on his thrusting shaft, saying, "Well, when rape is inevitable, as they say. Hmm, there's more to you than meets the eye when you have your pants on. But what about my Jim?"

"Merde alors, my sweet, anyone can tell you that when they turn yellow like that but refuse to vomit black, they are done for. Forget the poor specimen of a Puritan. Now that I know you better, I see the marriage would have been a disaster in any case. Mon Dieu, are you always this responsive?"

She moaned. "Oh, will you please stop talking and just *fuck* me?" I'm coming!"

So he did, and when they came up for air at last, Martha sighed, and said, "Oh, this is so confusing. I thought if I wasn't Jim's girl I was Dick's."

Gaston started moving in her again to keep it up as he said, "Dick has a girl, and he refuses to share her, the selfish child. If you don't want a large female Basque pulling your red hair out by the fistful, all the way back to Limón, you had etter resign yourself to being *my* girl, for now. Don't worry, we shall probably be tired of each other by the time we disembark. So you won't be stuck with a dirty old man."

She moved her hips teasingly and pleaded, "Would you stick me faster, you dirty old man?"

Back at the old Spanish fort, El Criado Publico moaned with the pain of the effort as he struck a match to find out where in the hell he was. His legs were pinned under a heavy beam. A candlestick from the rooms above was half-buried in the thick plaster dust near enough to reach. So he managed to light the wick before the match went out. The candle burned brightly on its side on the cellar floor. The old man tried to sit up. He managed only to prop himself up on one elbow as he gazed about in dismay. He saw that by some miracle the falling wreckage had formed a sort of cave around him and the beam pinning him to the stone floor. At one end of the sealed-in cavern, or tomb, his daughter, Inocencia, seemed to be peeking like an elf at him over other beams. Her eyes were staring blankly at him. He asked "Are you still alive, you wicked child? I thought I saw you shot."

Inocencia didn't answer. He looked closer and saw that she wasn't really peeking over the debris at him. Her severed head was simply resting on its stump. There was surprisingly little blood, and her face looked more serene than it had been in recent memory.

He sighed and said, "Your death was swifter than what I'd had in mind. Attempted patricide calls for stern justice, my child. But what is done is done. In all justice, I may as well confess that your rebellious nature may have been at least partly a product of my own mistakes in rearing you. As I told that prisoner we left to enjoy the flesh of his own dead mother, a parent must bear some responsibility for a wayward child."

He heard movement in the darkness beyond the dim light of the candle. It sounded like digging. He shouted, "In here! I am trapped in here! Get me out and I shall reward you with a promotion, whoever you are!"

Ther was no answer, but the digging noises continued. They sounded hesitant. As if whoever it was was injured or confused. Zagal tried to remember who could be left. He knew Numero Uno was dead. Numero Segundo had taken a pistol shot in his own head after treacherously blowing off Numero Uno's face. Could it be that big Americano? Captain Gringo had demateralized as if my magic in the chaos of the gunfight over the dinner table upstairs. Criado Publico shouted, "Listen, forget what I said about treason, señor! That other Americano was probably delirious, as you suggested, eh? Get me out of here and all will be forgiven! I will see you get your pardon. Without me, there will *be* no pardon! So be swift and dig me out, you big ape!"

Powdered plaster and stone dust cascaded to the already dusty floor as the black jaguar, Diablo, poked a dusty muzzle through to El Criado Publico's side. Zagal gasped as the big cat wormed its whole head through to stare at him with glowing feline eyes. The old man gulped and said, "Nice kitty. Good kitty. You *are* a good kitty, no?"

The big cat wriggled in to join the trapped man and the severed head of its mistress, purring deep in its throat. Diablo was covered with dust and looked more gray than black as he moved slowly over, caught the scent of blood, and ignored the pinned-down man to pad over to Inocencia's head and sniff it. The mingled scent of her blood and perfume confused the already confused jaguar's instincts. It reclined by the head and raised a furry hind leg to lick at his big pink penis. But his mistress did seem to want to mate with him, for some reason, and Diablo had other appetites. They hadn't fed him properly in that dark place they'd been keeping him, so he was hungry.

He sniffed at the blood in the air of the stuffy cavern, or tomb. It never occurred to the big cat to taste the flesh of the dead girl who'd been such a loving mistress indeed. But Diablo had to eat *something*.

He moved over to the dead girl's pinned-down father, regarding Zagal with the same expression as a housecat investigating a trapped mouse. The old man whimpered, "No! For the love of God, not that!"

But it was to be that, he learned to his horror, as the jaguar lowered its big belly to the floor at his side and began to eat him, without bothering to kill him first.

Back aboard the *Nombre Nada*; Captain Gringo had been thinking about that promised pardon, too, rather wistfully. It had probably been pie in the sky, and a guy had to do what a guy had to do, but he sure could have used it. He and Gaston still had the front money, and Esperanza had some nice arms to peddle at a profit as well, but he still felt mighty homesick.

He felt less so when Esperanza nudged him in the ribs on the rainswept stern deck and said, "Bueno. We are safely out to sea at last and don't have to worry about gunboats in this storm. Why don't we go to my quarters and get out of these wet clothes and into each other, eh?"

He agreed that her suggestion beat standing in the rain. So they locked themselves in and undressed calmly, as old friends tended to.

But their friendship began to warm indeed as they tumbled naked into Esperanza's clean linens together. She said, "Madre de Dios! Your poor cock is cold as ice."

He laughed and said it wasn't any colder than her bare nipples as he mounted her. Her big thighs were cold too, as she hugged his naked hips with them and gasped, "Ay, que frio!" as he slid his cold erection into warmer climes indeed. She clamped down with her hot pink internal delights and in no time at all they were both not only warmed up but sweating a bit. He reached down and pulled a sheet over them to keep them from winding up with pneumonia when and if they ever stopped.

They didn't for quite some time. As Esperanza took charge by getting on top, she laughed down at him and said, "I see you were faithful to me ashore, this time. What kept you out of that redhead and crazy Zagal's crazy daughter, eh?"

He didn't like to lie to his friends, so he said, "The last time I noticed Gaston, *he* had the redhead bound for glory. Inocencia just wasn't my type, I guess. Did you know she was a real animal lover?"

Esperanza leaned forward to tease his face with her swaying nipples as she moved sensuously on his shaft, saying, "Well, I noticed she seemed very fond of that black jaguar and . . . oh, you mean she was *that* kind of an animal lover?"

"Yeah. Went in for incest, too. Gaston got it out of her, not me. Like I said, she just wasn't my type."

"I'm glad. Could I get on the bottom again, por favor? I can't move as fast as you and I'm almost there again."

He rolled her politely on her back, hooked an elbow under each of her knees to hold her long legs spread high, and proceeded to pound her good until they'd both climaxed again, hard.

As he collapsed atop her, Esperanza hugged him to her

ample breasts and crooned, "Oh, I am glad indeed. I saved up for this by neglecting my cabin boy, this voyage. I was hoping you'd be this nice to me, Dick. But, knowing you, I was afraid you'd have made love to at least a dozen other women before I got back."

He chuckled and mused aloud, "As a matter of fact, there were hardly any dames at all around, this time. Remind me never to sign up with a celibate order again. They didn't even have the usual adelitas. So for once Gaston and I just had to behave ourselves."

Then he rolled her on her face to remount her from behind as he muttered to himself, "Oh, well, maybe the next outfit we join will be more interesting."